SECND NATURE

"OK, lads," Commander Schreck said to his crewmen. "There's no time like the present, is there? Let 'em drop."

Ten pairs of hands operated five different sets of launching commands, punching in the secret codes which would engage the bombs which the battlecruiser carried in its belly.

There was a whirring of mechanisms, and slowly the underside of the ship opened to reveal five stubby torpedoes. At this command from Schreck, the missiles were launched, hurtling down into Pasiphae's atmosphere.

Schreck barked another command, and the ship engaged its sub-tachyon drive, and sped away from the planetoid at approximately one twentieth of the speed of light.

When Pasiphae exploded in a brilliant cloud of nuclear energy, Commander Schreck was already halfway back to Mars.

Also in the Point SF series:

Look out for:

SECOND NATURE

Nigel Robinson

■■SCHOLASTIC

Scholastic Children's Books,
Commonwealth House, 1–19 New Oxford Street,
London WC1A 1NU, UK
a division of Scholastic Ltd
London ~ New York ~ Toronto ~ Sydney ~ Auckland

Published in the UK by Scholastic Ltd, 1996

Copyright © Nigel Robinson, 1996

ISBN 0 590 55837 4

Typeset by DP Photosetting, Aylesbury, Bucks.
Printed by Cox & Wyman Ltd, Reading, Berks.

10 9 8 7 6 5 4 3 2 1

CONTENTS

The Magnificent Donovan Trueheart

Somewhere in the great interplanetary night, where starlight itself grows cold and the only sound is the deafening rush of silence, the Island hung, a sleek and gleaming bio-station, an artificial satellite over five kilometres, or klicks, in length, and yet home to a little under six and a half thousand carefully selected individuals.

It spun slowly on its own axis, maintaining an almost equidistant position between two worlds, planets which it was constantly surveying, recording and evaluating. A long time ago, even before the technology needed to construct the Island had been developed, these planets had been known as Mars and Earth. Today, thousands of years later, they were called TerraNova and the Home Planet. To refer to them by any other name was an offence for which the only punishment was death: their former names were a relic of the Old Times, reminders of a time of chaos and inefficiency, of hardship and despair – in short, of the time before the System.

Stretching over four thousand million klicks, from the hell-planet, Mercury, to the great mining worlds of Uranus and Neptune, the System was a vast administration of twenty-one colonized worlds and one hundred billion souls. Formed in the aftermath of the Great Colonial Wars of the twenty-second and twenty-third centuries, it ruled its citizens with a hand of the strongest titanium, wrapped up in a glove of the finest insulatory fabric. The System organized everything for you from the day you were born to the day you were terminated. It decided what career you should pursue (all for the greater good of the System, of course); which person you would be pair-bonded with for the rest of your life; and even the number of children you were allowed to have. The System had once even tried (unsuccessfully, it has to be allowed) to dictate which method you should employ to conceive your children, whether it be the natural way, or through one of the many test-tube, DNA-grafting or cloning processes which had been developed by the end of the twenty-first century. And if you obeyed the System's commands, then it made sure that all your needs were provided for.

And it was starving, the System President reflected

ironically, as he munched idly on a leg of lamb, cooked in a rich cream and mushroom sauce, while studying the reports he had just called up on the holo-screen in the centre of his antique mahogany desk. (Mahogany was a by-product of trees, so people had told him; the President hadn't seen a tree since his childhood, but he looked back on them with a certain fondness.)

The Magnificent Donovan Trueheart – for that was the name of the System President – frowned, and a black look crossed his face: the lamb was far too fatty! Didn't these damn cooks know any better? After all, his waistline wasn't as trim as it used to be. Resigning himself philosophically to his new diet, he tossed the half-eaten leg of lamb over his shoulder where it was instantly pounced upon by Gabriel, his pet lupe.

A *lupus leonis*, a creature genetically engineered from cells taken from a wolf and a lion (before the big cats became extinct about fifty years ago, of course), Gabriel only sniffed curiously at the piece of meat before turning his snout up at it in disgust. The lamb had been killed all of an hour ago in the special breeding pens on board the Island; Gabriel was used to much fresher meat than that, meat through which living blood still coursed. With a grunt, he resumed his customary place at his master's feet.

The Trueheart sipped at his glass of fine red wine (a '21 Premier Cru, from the Olympus vineyards on TerraNova), and licked his lips appreciatively.

Donovan Trueheart loved the good things in life – fine clothes, fine food and fine furnishings like the expensive carpets and luxurious velvet drapes in his office – but it had been a piece of inspired genius on his part to transform the foothills of Olympus Mons into vineyards. They were reserved exclusively for his own use, of course; if the common people were allowed wines such as these, who knew what manner of thoughts they might dare to think?

The Trueheart operated a touch-sensitive control by the side of his desk, and there was a discreet swish of velvet as the drapes at the far end of the room parted and a finely polished oak door opened (the Trueheart hadn't seen an oak tree for years either). Donovan Trueheart beamed with delight, and stood up to welcome his visitor.

"Aha, the Child Roland!" he said, in a thin and reedy voice, and marched forward to shake the newcomer's hand. "As punctual as ever!"

"I would not dream of being late for any appointment with Your Magnificence," the Child Roland said graciously, and accepted the Trueheart's offer of a place on his sofa. Although the Child looked much younger, he was, in fact, in his late twenties, and with his muscular figure, wild raven hair and steel-blue eyes, he seemed the complete opposite of Trueheart.

Roland's face possessed the sort of sensitivity and wide-eyed playfulness that had already broken many women's hearts, while the Trueheart's once-handsome features were now jowly, his good-looks twisted and scarred by the cruelties he had inflicted over the past forty years, the last three of which he had spent as System President. In fact, at times it seemed that the only thing the two men shared was a love of exquisite clothes. Roland invariably dressed in spotlessly white tunics and trousers, tied at the waist by a band of bright-blue velvet in order to accentuate his trim figure; the Trueheart had taken to wearing loose and heavy scarlet robes, in an attempt to disguise his ever-increasing midriff.

The Trueheart walked over to his desk and poured out another glass of wine, which he handed to Roland. Before sipping it, Roland swirled the liquid around, checking its colour in the room's subdued lighting (so different from the harsh fluorescence of the rest of the space station), and extravagantly sniffed its bouquet.

"It's a fine wine, my Lord," he opined, after a moment's consideration. "An Olympus '21, I believe?"

The Trueheart beamed. "Indeed!" he said, happily. "It's a joy to have a man such as you for my trusted advisor and aide-de-camp, Roland. Most of the other dolts who work for the System couldn't tell an Olympus from ditchwater!"

"I try to be conversant in everything that is of interest to the Trueheart," Roland said, obsequiously. In actual fact, he detested the taste of alcohol. "But particularly dear to my heart have always been the wines of Mars...'

The Trueheart's face suddenly darkened and a dangerous glint appeared in his green eyes; Roland felt his throat tighten as he realized his mistake.

"My Lord, I didn't mean..."

"The planet is called TerraNova," the Trueheart said, frostily. "To call it by its ancient name is to invite summary execution upon oneself."

"It was merely a slip of the tongue, Your Magnificence," Roland said, and experienced a momentary twinge of panic. "I assure you it will not happen again..."

Donovan Trueheart glared at his advisor for a long time. And then his face relaxed, and he smiled, and he put an avuncular arm around Roland's shoulders.

"Don't let it trouble you, my son," the Trueheart said, kindly. "You are my trusted protégé, the student I myself picked out of the Academy and promoted into my personal staff. Men such as you or I can speak freely: we have no need of rules..."

"I am grateful to the Trueheart," Roland said, relaxing. However, the point had been made: Donovan Trueheart had the power of life or death over everyone, including even those who were his most trusted advisors.

The Trueheart clapped his hands, like a schoolteacher rallying his class to order. "Now, down to business," he said. "You have your reports?"

"Of course," Roland smiled, and took out from his tunic his personal "smart-box". The height of System technology, it was an ebony-coloured box, little more than a centimetre thick and small enough to fit into the palm of his hand. It gave Roland access to every single cybernetic intelligence within the System, from the kilometre-long bio-computers on board the Island, to the tiniest holo-decks in the furthest outposts of the System. Roland's fingers dashed speedily over its surface, and a stream of coded figures appeared on its tiny scanner.

"Food production is dropping on TerraNova," he announced, and then caught the encouraging glint in the Trueheart's eyes. "On *Mars*, I mean," he said with a smile.

"The reason?" the Trueheart demanded, now all business-like.

"Pollution of the soil, breaking down of the artificial ozone layer, a thousand and one things," Roland replied, without a hint of feeling or regret. "It seems our industries down there were pumping out more effluent than we imagined – we've poisoned half the planet."

The Trueheart stroked his beardless chin thoughtfully. "Just as our ancestors did on Earth," he said, and then grinned conspiratorially at Roland. "On the Home Planet, I mean, of course!" A worrying thought struck him. "The vineyards around Olympus Mons..."

"Perfectly safe, Your Magnificence," Roland reassured him. "I personally made sure of that."

"Thank the System for that, then," the Trueheart said, and breathed a heartfelt sigh of relief. He made a mental note to order a case of wine for the Child Roland by way of thanks; or rather half a crate – it wouldn't do to give the young and ambitious man too many ideas. "Immediate consequence of the food shortages?" he demanded.

Roland consulted his smart-box again. "Four billion-plus out of a planet population of eight point three-five billion living at starvation level," he reported coolly, and then added helpfully: "That's almost half the planet."

"The *political* consequences, I mean!" the Trueheart said wearily; Roland did have a tendency to bore him with trivialities sometimes.

"Stirrings of discontent amongst the general populace," he read off. "Talk of revolt. Strikes at several workplaces."

"Solution?"

"The ringleaders are due to be –" Roland considered his words carefully, so as not to offend the Trueheart's legendary sensibilities – " 'removed'. You will have nothing to fear from them again. And as for their followers they will be allocated new jobs in the Happy Camps."

"Excellent!" the Trueheart said. "Some forced labour for the greater glory of the System will do them good – instil some backbone and discipline into them!''

"Of course, Your Magnificence," Roland agreed. The Happy Camps were one of the Child's own ideas, rehabilitation centres and teaching establishments in which those dissatisfied with the System's way of life were "offered" the opportunity to learn the error of their ways, while at the same time doing some helpful "community work". Few returned.

"What about repercussions from the disappearances?" the Trueheart asked. "Won't people ask questions?"

"Allow me to deal with that, Your Magnificence," the Child Roland reassured him. "As your Minister for Information and Enlightenment, I think you can rely on me to invent a suitable explanation. And, of course, anyone who dares to think the unthinkable and doubt the truth of that explanation can join their colleagues in the Happy Camps."

"How could I ever doubt you, Roland?" the Trueheart said. "You have served me faithfully for almost three years now, ever since –" the Trueheart ground his teeth, as he was reminded of a painful memory – "ever since that witch and her two friends escaped – I mean, relocated elsewhere..."

"If the post of Minister for Information and Enlightenment had been created then, I'm sure the news of their 'relocation' could have been contained," the Child Roland agreed. "But when the daughter of a top-ranking Government scientist relocates from TerraNova..."

"...taking with her two friends, and stealing a skimmer under the noses of our guards and top-security cameras..." the Trueheart added.

"Most of the cameras were being used to record Your Magnificence's official birthday celebrations," Roland reminded him.

The Trueheart regarded Roland balefully, but chose not to comment on his last remark. "Ever since then, those three renegades have been a thorn in my side, a constant reminder that there are ingrates in the System who do not love me with all their heart." The Trueheart placed a hand over his breast, as though his heart was breaking. "Some even say that they have become symbols for discontented young people throughout the System, that holo-images of them are used to decorate student quarters in the Academy..."

"Use of such images is punishable by termination," the Child Roland reminded him. "But I do not quite understand why Your Magnificence has allowed the three of them to live for so long. After all, we know which planet they are on..."

"I allow them to live because the time is not yet right for them to die," the Trueheart said. He looked warily at the Child Roland. "How much can I trust you, Roland?" he asked.

"With your very being."

The Trueheart grunted, and called up another

image on the holo-screen. A stream of complex figures appeared, followed by a succession of charts, representations of the human body and brain-pattern scans. The Child Roland affected ignorance.

"I do not understand, Your Magnificence," he lied. "What do these things all mean?"

"They are the medical records of Shari Sharifi, Kristas Chernenko and their damnable friend, Cruse," the Trueheart said, and snapped off the image, before the Child Roland had a chance to study them too carefully. "They have told me much, Roland..."

Without explaining further, Donovan Trueheart stood up and walked over to the far wall, where he pulled back the drapes covering a huge transparent screen, revealing the view outside the Island Space Station. There, far off in the distance, shone a steady blue pin-prick of light: the Home Planet, the planet Earth from which all human life had evolved over a million years ago.

Once it had been a green and teeming land; now it was a blighted cinder in space, its only inhabitants hideous mutations of the human form, and the Non-Persons, those rebels and bandits who had escaped the System and were eking out a miserable existence on the surface of that long-dead world.

"The System has become too successful, too generous," the Trueheart said, musing aloud. "For much too long we have cosseted those we are sworn to protect until they have become like children, unable to fend for themselves. And like children, when things go wrong, they turn against their providers..."

Roland nodded sympathetically. "The Martian riots were relatively easy for me to suppress," he said. "But unrest is growing on the outer worlds too. Some have even dared to speak out against you, Your Magnificence, demanding that you should resign from the Presidency in favour of a younger man, for someone who can put food into their mouths, and restore the gas mines of Jupiter and Saturn to their former glory and productivity."

In fact, the Child Roland's name had been put forward (against his will, of course) as a possible successor to the Trueheart on the unthinkable day when he might have to retire. Roland chose not to mention that fact.

The Trueheart spun round, and marched angrily up to Roland. He grabbed the young man by the collar of his tunic, and dragged him roughly to his feet.

"Don't you think I don't know that!" he barked, his face white with rage. "Don't you think that I don't know how precarious my position is? And do you seriously believe I intend to stand by and do nothing while the whole of the System falls about me into chaos and decline?"

"I assure you that you have the full support of all the members of the Board," Roland said, referring to the System's governing body.

The Trueheart pushed Roland down on to the sofa.

"But it is not enough!" he said, and placed a hand over his heart. "I need the people to respect me once more, Roland! And I need them also to fear me! To know that there is nothing they can do, no treacherous words they can utter, no rebellious thoughts they can harbour without my knowing it, nothing they can do without my express permission!"

Roland sat up and smoothed the creases in his tunic, trying to regain some of his dignity. "A show trial perhaps, Your Magnificence?" he suggested. "I can round up the usual suspects. We could say that they were co-conspirators in a plot to end Your Magnificence's life...'

The Trueheart smiled a tiny, twisted smile, which sent shudders down Roland's spine. "Not this time, I think, Roland," he said softly, and invited the young man to join him by the window. He pointed down at the blue light shining in the blackness.

"Our answer lies down there, my child," he said wistfully, and not for the first time Roland was taken aback by the Trueheart's abrupt change of mood.

"The Home Planet, Your Magnificence?" Roland asked. "But it is a dead world where nothing can survive – apart from the Mutes, of course, and they're of no consequence..."

"On the contrary," the Trueheart said, and his eyes gleamed with an almost Messianic gleam. He looked deep into Roland's eyes: it was a gaze which shook Roland to the very core of his being. "It is many centuries since our ancestors left our home world, and the Earth has had time to recover from their excesses. Food is lacking there, but it does exist. Most rivers run foul and polluted, but there are some that can be drunk from and will produce only slight illness." He smiled. "Sometimes I even think that there is another force at work, fighting back, ensuring that the land will grow again..."

"Your Magnificence?" The Child Roland didn't like the sound of this one little bit.

"And then I remind myself that I am the Great Donovan Trueheart and that there is no one more powerful than me," the Trueheart said, and then added, almost as an afterthought: "Tell me, Roland, have you ever heard of God?"

Roland frowned, trying to remember his lessons at the Academy. "It's an old legend, isn't it?" he asked. "An unsubstantiated notion of a spurious universal truth, designed as an emotional and psychic crutch for those who should know better. A harmless superstition, nothing more..."

"Countless centuries ago, even men such as you or me believed in one universal power," the Trueheart said. "A being capable of creating life out of the dust, a being to be feared just as much as it was to be loved and obeyed."

"The Trueheart's learning is indeed wide," Roland said.

"I'm merely a most voracious reader, Roland," the

Trueheart said, self-deprecatingly. "I read it in a book once – you do know what a book is, don't you?"

The Trueheart sighed when the Child Roland said that he did indeed know what a book was, and considered it a clumsy, untidy and outmoded way of storing data: the youth of today, the Trueheart reflected, no longer had any soul. He drew the drapes closed, and returned to the sofa to reclaim his unfinished glass of wine.

"I am the System President, with the power of life and death over every one of my subjects," he stated airily. "But I grow tired of that, Roland. I long for other challenges, other adventures. . ."

"Your Magnificence?" Roland wasn't quite sure what he was hearing. Was the Trueheart actually going to resign, and give up all his power? And if so, where would the Child Roland stand in the new order of things?

"There are more important things than just being the most powerful man in the history of the System," the Trueheart said. "You know, Roland, I think that I would rather like to be God!"

And with that the Trueheart dismissed his aide-de-camp. As the Child Roland left his master's presence, he knew that Donovan Trueheart was either the greatest and most visionary genius who had ever lived – or he was totally and irretrievably insane.

Funeral for a Friend

Standing by the edge of the ocean, Shari Sharifi looked up at the tiny lights criss-crossing the ochre-coloured sky and sighed. A long time ago, she knew, that sky would have been blue, speckled with fluffy white clouds, and crowded with flocks of migrating birds. Now every bird was long extinct, and what few clouds remained in the sky hung black and threatening, bearing not life-giving water but acid rain.

Once the beach she was standing on would have been made of silvery-white sand rather than brown sludge; and the sea would have tanged of salt and spray, rather than sulphur and carbon monoxide. If there had ever been a hell, Shari reflected, then it could not have been worse than the planet Earth. It was a wonder that she and her friends could even survive in this wasteland. But, as Donovan Trueheart himself had said, some hardy crops did grow here; not all waters were irrevocably polluted; and the air, although filthy and thin, was also breathable, as long as you wore an oxy-mask for at least part of each day. Planet Earth wasn't dead, Shari realized; on the other hand, it wasn't exactly in the best of health.

Shari tensed as she suddenly became aware of someone creeping up behind her. She intuited the presence of her would-be attacker, rather than heard it, and she steeled her body, ready to defend herself.

In one slow, and deceptively casual movement, she let her hand drop to her belt and the zip-gun which always hung from it. Her fingers brushed against it, accidentally; or so it seemed.

Relax, she told herself, *let them think that you don't know they're there; and then, at the very last second—*

She spun around, whipped the zip-gun out of its holster, and aimed it at the stranger.

And then relaxed, smiled, and returned the gun to its holster.

"Cruse!" she said, shaking her head reprovingly. "What do you think you're up to – sneaking up on me like that?"

The swarthy young man, with the lank dark hair and coal-black eyes, grinned his usual crooked grin, revealing yellowing and chipped front teeth. "Your reflexes are improving," he congratulated her.

"Three years ago you wouldn't have moved as fast as that."

"I had to learn," she said, and there was a trace of sadness in her voice, and a pained expression on her pretty face, whose complexion betrayed her East Asiatic ancestry, a land which had been nuked out of existence almost five hundred years ago. "One second's hesitation on this planet, and you're dead meat. You taught me that."

"It's the law of wastelands – kill or be killed," Cruse agreed. "The survival of the fittest." Then he sneered, although not unkindly. "Life outside the System isn't quite the freewheeling paradise you thought it would be, is it?"

Shari nodded up at the sky. "It's still better than what's out there," she said. "Twenty-one moons and planets where you're told what to do from the day you are born, right up to the day those faceless bureaucrats decide how and when you die. And heaven help you if you dare to say 'no', or even ask the question 'why?'."

"There are lots of people in the System who are happy with their lives," Cruse said. "Lots of people perfectly content with their lot."

"Maybe so," said Shari, and ran long fingers through her unkempt short, black hair in a vain effort to keep it tidy: hairdressers were an unheard-of luxury on what was left of planet Earth in the thirty-third century. "But do you know something really weird,

Cruse? I prefer to be unhappy. You and I know how corrupt the System is. I don't want to be part of a society which murders its own citizens as casually as you'd trample on a worm. That's why we stole a skimmer and escaped from it in the first place."

"To see the Universe, I think you said," Cruse reminded her and gestured at the panorama behind them: a vast and unpleasant wasteland of rock, slag and clinker, shrouded with the smell of death, through which meandered poisonous and noxious streams. He coughed: he hadn't used his oxy-mask for several hours now. "Not much of a beauty spot, is it?"

Shari smiled. She'd been so naïve when she'd asked the erstwhile mercenary to help her escape first her home world of Pasiphae, (one of the moons of Jupiter), and then TerraNova, dreaming of coursing the spaceways with him, a pair of happy-go-lucky rebels off to see the wonders of the Universe.

Unauthorised travel off-planet was strictly forbidden, and the moment they had reached inter-planetary space they had been attacked by the hunter-ships of Donovan Trueheart's crack squads. The stolen skimmer in which they had been travelling had been badly damaged, and it was only due to Cruse's flying skills that they had finally evaded their pursuers, and crash-landed here on the Home Planet, the world they insisted on calling Earth, by way of rebellion against the laws of the System.

They had been here for almost three years now, and, although Cruse had managed to repair most of the skimmer, its sub-tachyon drive, which provided them with the technology to travel off-planet, was damaged beyond repair. They were stranded on this dead planet now, the hell-world which had once been the birthplace for the entire human race.

"Perhaps things will grow here again – one day," she said wistfully, although she wasn't too sure that she believed it herself. "More trees and flowers, and enough crops to live on. Maybe the waters will run pure again, and we'll be able to drink it without adding de-tox tablets to it first."

Cruse laughed cynically, as he always did when Shari dared to think of better times. "And maybe Donovan Trueheart will grant us all a full and unconditional pardon!"

Shari looked up at the streaks of light in the sky. "There are more of his hunter-ships up there every day," she said apprehensively. "What are they doing orbiting the Earth? What are they looking for?"

Cruse shrugged. "Killing off as many Mutes as they can find, I suppose," he guessed, in a voice which betrayed no emotion. "The System doesn't like the failed results of their genetic experiments wandering around the place with nowhere to go. Gives the old Home Planet a bad name. That's probably why they gave up genetic experimentation completely about ten years ago."

"You told me about that," Shari said. "All of a sudden they just stopped. Why should that be?"

Cruse shrugged. "Knowledge of their existence was stirring up anti-System feeling, I suppose," he said. "But then that's never stopped Trueheart before."

"Especially now that he has the Child Roland," Shari remarked, and remembered the Minister for Information and Enlightenment's handsome face, from when she and Cruse had tapped into System video broadcasts. "If there's anyone who can stamp out any unrest in the System, then it's him."

Cruse stroked his stubbled chin. "It's just not like Trueheart to give up on something like that," he said.

"Why can't they just leave the mutants alone?" Shari asked, not expecting an answer from the older man. "The System dumped them here in the first place, to eke out a life as best as they could. So why go to the trouble of killing them now?"

"You ever seen a dead Mute, Shari?" Cruse asked pointedly, and Shari frowned.

"Of course I have," she said. "I've seen their bodies, shot by the System StormTroopers and left to rot."

Cruse shook his head. "I mean, *recently*," he corrected himself. This time Shari shook her head. "I have. Remember that time a couple of months ago, when we helped fly a group of Mutes to — what did you call those islands up north?"

"The Shetlands," Shari told him. "Way back in the twenty-second century they formed part of a country called Scottish Oil."

"Never heard of the place," Cruse said. "But then you were always the ancient history major at the Academy, not me. Anyway, remember the trouble we had making that flight—"

"Of course," Shari said, and shuddered. She and Cruse had been transporting in the partially-repaired skimmer a group of five mutants to the far-off islands, where they imagined they'd be safe from Donovan Trueheart's people, when they had been attacked by System security. In the subsequent skirmish Shari had been separated from her companions, and, when they had been reunited, one of the mutants had gone missing – a fifteen-year-old girl called Ara, who was charming and attractive, despite having all her limbs mutilated at the hands of one of the System's bio-geneticists.

"Ara died in that attack," Cruse told her.

"We never found her body," Shari pointed out. Even after three hard years on Earth she still found the thought of death unpleasant, unlike Cruse who often seemed to relish it.

"You wouldn't," Cruse said, matter-of-factly. "And there's a reason why you've never seen a dead Mute recently – the same reason why there are more and more of Trueheart's hunter-ships in the skies—"

"I wish you wouldn't call them 'Mutes', Cruse,"

Shari reproved him. "That's a System word. They're mutants – people just like you and me, who were unfortunate enough to be experimented on by the System bio-engineers. . ."

Cruse chuckled, clearly unimpressed by Shari's well-meant attempt at political correctness. "Mutes, mutants, it's all the same to me," he said casually. Shari glared at him.

"I was hiding behind a rock and there was nothing I could do to save Ara being shot down dead by the System troopers," Cruse continued. "And I saw what happened to her next. . ."

Shari looked curiously at Cruse, urging him to continue.

"I didn't tell you at the time," he said. "We've been through a lot together, but you're still not quite as hard as you'd like to think you are. . ."

"What is it, Cruse?" Shari demanded to know, praying that he wasn't going to tell her what she already half-suspected. "What didn't you want to tell me? What happened to Ara's body?"

"The System is *hungry*, Shari," he said in a cold monotone. "There isn't enough food on its twenty-one worlds to support its population any-more. Synthetic foodstuffs are all very well, but the food-factories can't keep up with demand. Any piece of fresh meat is welcome. . ."

He didn't need to say more, and Shari shivered

involuntarily. "Ara..." she finally said, in sheer disbelief. "They couldn't ... they wouldn't..."

"Like I said, any piece of meat is welcome, Shari," Cruse murmured darkly. "And the human body provides a pretty juicy source of protein..."

Shari turned sharply away, unwilling to listen further. "That's horrible!" she said. "And you seem to take some sort of sick and twisted pleasure in telling me!"

"It's life, Shari," Cruse said sadly. "And whatever you think, I don't enjoy telling you about some of this planet's more sordid facts of life..."

Shari turned back to look at Cruse: there were tears in her eyes which she brushed quickly away. "You said I've changed," she reminded him. "I'm not the little rich girl who hired you all those years ago to take me away from the System."

Cruse smiled, a half-smile which Shari couldn't decide was patronizing or not. "You're tougher, your reflexes are much sharper, I'll grant you that," he said, and Shari could detect a touch of admiration in his voice. "But you still trust people too much, you still believe in people's essential goodness..."

"Meaning you don't?" Shari accused him.

"Meaning that before I met you I was on the run from the System for almost ten years, living on my wits."

"You were a mercenary and a smuggler," Shari reminded him. "A gun for hire."

Cruse shrugged nonchalantly: his criminal past held no shame for him. "I had to survive," he said simply. "And while I was out there surviving I learnt to trust no one. People will shoot you in the back for a cup of unpolluted water, or a slice of decontaminated fresh meat – Mute or otherwise. So I shoot first."

"Trust no one?" Shari repeated Cruse's words. "Does that mean that you don't trust me? Or Kristas?" Cruse remained silent and Shari considered Cruse through narrow, accusing eyes. "So there's no room for love? No room for self-sacrifice or helping out one's fellow human beings?"

Now it was Cruse who turned away. "Why should there be?" he shrugged awkwardly.

There were a few seconds of silence between them, as Shari wondered whether to point out to Cruse that helping other people had been exactly what he had been doing for the past three years. Instead she said softly, "You still miss her, don't you?"

Cruse looked up into the sky, watching the trail of one of the hunter-ships as it veered off towards the north. "Miss who?" he said.

"Marla," Shari said, and laid a friendly hand on Cruse's broad shoulders. He let it rest there. Trusting her.

"Marla is dead, and has been dead for ten years now," he said finally. "Slaughtered by Trueheart and his scum, for daring to speak out against the System.

They called her 'Mad' Marla, but there was nothing insane about her. All she wanted was a just and fair world for all – a world where Mutes aren't treated as outcasts or as a convenient source of food, a world where people are equal and can decide their own future rather than have it dictated to them by the System."

Shari nodded wisely. Although she hadn't known them at that time, she was aware that, as teenagers, Cruse and Marla had been deeply in love. When Marla had been murdered, Cruse had changed from an idealistic teenager to the cold, ruthless and occasionally brutal man standing before her. Yet there were still traces of the old Cruse: otherwise why was he helping to protect the mutants from Donovan Trueheart's troops? Indeed, why was he still staying with her? He had claimed that he would leave her once he was certain that she could look after herself on this planet, but she didn't believe that for one second. Cruse, like everyone else sooner or later in this life, had come to the conclusion that he needed to belong somewhere, to someone.

Not that they were lovers. There was a time when Shari naïvely imagined that she and Cruse might have made a couple, like those in the old-fashioned story books she had read back home on Pasiphae, one of the terraformed moons of Jupiter. It was there that she had first met him, and recognized in him his essential humanity which he always tried so hard to conceal.

26

But she had soon realized that they would only ever be friends, for the memory of "Mad" Marla's death was still fresh in his memory, even ten years after the event. Indeed, if anything could be claimed to rule Cruse's life, or provide him with his *raison d'être*, then it was his love for the long-dead Marla, and for the things Marla stood for.

And one other thing too, Shari realized, as Cruse turned back to her, his face set and hard, a mask concealing his emotions. *His hatred for the man who killed "Mad" Marla*. If Donovan Trueheart was here now, then Cruse would rip the tyrant's "true" heart from out of his very breast.

Shari hugged herself for warmth: the sun was sinking below the horizon, and night would soon fall, bringing with it its sub-zero temperatures. It was time to return to their temporary encampment in the valley over the next rise. There they would be safe from the cold, and the wild beasts which prowled the area at night, as well as the other creatures she preferred not to think about. But before that there was one final thing she had to do.

She smiled weakly and waved, as she saw a figure tramping over the crest of the rocky hill towards her and Cruse. The newcomer was silhouetted in the moonlight and Shari saw that over his shoulders he was carrying a large spade; his bare, muscular arms were covered with earth and mud. He walked up to them, and gave Cruse a perfunctory nod, before addressing Shari.

"It's ready," he said. "Let's get it over with quickly, shall we?"

"Thanks, Kristas," Shari said. "I really appreciate it."

Kristas shrugged off her thanks. "It was the least I could do," he said. "She was my friend as well. . ."

By Shari's side Cruse chuckled cynically. "She was a blasted monkey, that's all!" he said. "A blasted monkey that just upped and died!"

Shari found herself glaring once more at Cruse. "Doob was my pet!" she snapped at him. "And she deserves to be buried properly!"

"A waste of time and energy," Cruse said off-handedly. "We could be out looking for food. And Kristas could put himself to much better use than digging a grave for a pet. Although at least it's put a few muscles on him – I remember how weedy he was when I first met him."

Shari felt her blood rise. She knew that Cruse had been fond of the monkey too, so why was he pretending the animal's death didn't matter to him? Why would he never allow himself to pull down those blasted defences of his, and show some genuine emotion for a change? She was about to say something to him, when Kristas came between them. There was an angry look on his face, which twisted his normally soft features into an expression which was much more frightening.

"Look, can you two stop your bickering?" he demanded angrily. "It's getting dark, and the sooner we get back to our base camp then the happier I'm going to be. For tonight at least!"

"Tonight?" asked Curse. "What d'you mean?"

Kristas frowned. "I'm not sure," he said. "I've got a feeling, that's all..."

"A feeling!" Cruse sneered. "You know, Kristas, I'd thought you'd grown up — but you're still the ineffectual little dreamer you always were!"

"You're just imagining things, Kristas," Shari said gently. "And if anything does happen we've all got our zip-guns."

Kristas smiled. "I guess you're right," he said, and glanced at Cruse. "Both of you." He started to move away, followed by Shari, who turned to look at Cruse.

"Are you coming?" she asked.

Cruse rammed his hands into the pockets of his combat fatigues, and grunted an affirmative reply. As he padded after them, Shari and Kristas exchanged a wry smile. Cruse had been as fond of Doob as Shari had, but he'd die before he let anyone know!

Kristas had dug a small hole just over the crest of the hill, beneath the branches of an old oak tree, which, amazingly, still bore a few leaves. It was a quiet place, surrounded on three sides by clumps of sun-scorched bushes; *a good place to be buried in*, thought Shari, *if anywhere on Earth can be called a good place.*

She looked down sadly at the emaciated body of her pet. It had been only three days ago that Doob had been happily scrambling amongst the bracken and scrub, foraging for seeds and berries, and now she was dead, struck down by a mysterious wasting illness. Cruse, who had acquired some basic medical knowledge on his travels, had attempted to save her, but in vain. Like the planet itself, Doob had seemed to give up all desire to live, and plague and contagion galloped across the face of the old home planet like a presager of the Apocalypse.

Shari wiped a tear from her eye, and smiled. "She looks at peace now, doesn't she?" She asked Kristas, but it was Cruse who replied.

"When you're dead, you're dead," he muttered, and hoped that neither of them would notice the small tear which had also appeared in the corner of his right eye. He looked across at Kristas who wasn't staring down at the grave – *and isn't bawling his eyes out like a little kid either,* Cruse thought uncharitably – but looking all around, his tear-free eyes darting this way and that. *As though he's looking for something,* Cruse realized.

Or someone. . .

"This is a solemn occasion," Cruse drawled sarcastically. "Can't you focus your attention on the damn chimp for a least a few seconds?"

"What?" Kristas's head jerked, as though Cruse had just awoken him from a deep sleep. He raised a hand to his forehead, brushing back his long blond hair from his eyes. "Sorry..." he said.

"Another of your headaches, Kristas?" Shari asked sympathetically. "You've been having quite a few of those lately..."

"I'm OK!" Kristas snapped, and then smiled awkwardly, before apologizing again. He stepped towards Doob's open grave, and, on Shari's command slowly started to shovel earth into the hole.

As he did so, Cruse watched him thoughtfully. Cruse considered himself a good judge of character – he had to be – but he had never been able to get the full measure of Kristas, and that worried him. The three of them had been together for a long time now, and had shared many experiences. He should trust Kristas – and most of the time he did. But there had always been something different about Kristas, something about him which Cruse couldn't quite fathom: an occasional dark look in his normally clear blue eyes which suggested that he was hiding something.

Despite what he had said earlier to Shari, Cruse did trust her and Kristas, in his own way, at least. If they had to survive, the three of them alone on a dangerous and abandoned planet, then they had to. But lately Kristas had been wandering off on his own, and, when asked where he had been, had always replied evasively. Cruse's trust was always hard-earned and Kristas's secrecy, coupled with these abrupt changes of mood, made Cruse wary. After all, Marla had "betrayed" him by getting herself killed; why should he trust someone who was the complete opposite of all that Cruse stood for. Cruse tried to put his doubts aside and turned his attention to Doob in the shallow grave. He wiped a further tear from his eye and hoped that no one had noticed.

"I'll miss her," Shari sighed, as Kristas shovelled the last clump of earth into the grave. "Why is it that everything must die on this planet? The plants, the trees, everything?"

Kristas laid down his shovel, and reached up to the low overhanging branches of the oak tree, and pulled off a leaf.

"Not everything dies, Shari," he said, and handed her the leaf. "Nature always wins through somehow. She's survived pestilence, radiation, even the System's pollution..."

"Only just," Shari corrected him.

"But the point is that she is surviving," Kristas insisted. "By the skin of her teeth, maybe. Where there's life there's hope – why, you never know, we might even see a flower one day..."

"Not in our lifetimes," Cruse said, and found that Kristas was no longer looking at him or Shari. His eyes were looking off to the north, a glimmer of anticipation in them.

Cruse marched up angrily to him. "Look, what's going on?" he demanded to know. "What – or who – are you looking—"

Several things happened at once. A flash of energy streaked past Cruse, and he pushed Kristas to the ground, where they both landed with a sickening *thud.* A hail of bullets pinged off the bark of the oak tree and Shari dived to her knees, whipping out her zip-gun, and aiming it ahead of her, ready to fire on their as yet unseen attackers. Cruse leapt to his feet, his gun already in his hand, as he heard the cries of their attackers trampling through the undergrowth towards them.

He glanced back at Shari. "Get back to camp!" he cried. "I'll hold them off!"

"I can't leave you!" she protested, and leapt back as another round of bullets exploded in the ground before her.

Kristas, who had staggered to his feet, pointed in the distance. There about twenty metres away, but gaining on them rapidly, was a group of six, black-clad, jackbooted and helmeted gunmen, the dreaded StormTroopers of Donovan Trueheart. Cruse raised his zip-gun and fired; one of them fell down dead and he yelped with triumph.

"Cruse! Run! You can't stay here shooting them!" Shari screamed, as she saw another StormTrooper fall down. The others were nearly upon them now: it seemed a miracle that they hadn't yet been hit by any of the flying bullets, particularly as the StormTroopers were notorious for being deadly crack-shots.

"There's only six of 'em!" Cruse laughed, as he launched another round of fire on the troopers.

"Oh no, there's not!" Kristas shouted, and pointed in the other direction. A second squad of ten or more Troopers were approaching them from behind. Within minutes they would all be surrounded.

"So start shooting them!" Cruse ordered.

"They're too many!" Kristas protested. "We have to get away!"

"You got any ideas?" Cruse snapped, and ducked as a bolt of energy from one of the StormTroopers' plasma rifles blazed above his head. "We're sitting ducks here!"

Kristas pointed to a rocky promontory further down the beach. Chalky-white cliffs rose from the sludgy sand. He ran down the hill and along the beach followed by Shari and Cruse.

"Up here!" he said, and was already cupping his hands to provide a foothold for Shari. "They won't follow us up here!"

"And how do you know that?" Cruse sneered, as he continued to try and hold off the approaching StormTroopers.

"For God's sake, Cruse, stop arguing, and climb up here," cried Shari who had scrabbled up to the top of the bluff. Kristas was starting to follow her, searching for hand- and foot-holds in the crumbling chalk-face.

Still the StormTroopers fired on them, and the rock exploded all around him, showering him with chalk and limestone.

Dragging himself over the edge, Kristas turned back and looked down at Cruse. The StormTroopers were almost upon him, and Kristas reached down his hand for him. Cruse grabbed it, and started to haul himself up the rock face.

One of the younger StormTroopers caught up with them, and threw himself on to Cruse, grabbing his legs, and started to drag him down. Cruse kicked out at him with his feet, but the Trooper was too strong. He pulled him down to the beach, and wrestled the zip-gun from Cruse's hand. They rolled around in the dirt and sludge, with the Trooper raining blows upon Cruse's face. As Cruse tried to throw him off he looked up at Kristas who was peering over the edge of the cliff.

"Shoot him, goddam you!" he cried.

On the cliff Kristas whipped the zip-gun out of his belt holster, and aimed. Cruse was laying prone on the ground, holding the Trooper on top of him: the thug would be an easy target. Taking a deep breath, Kristas prepared to squeeze the trigger.

And found he couldn't. His gun finger refused to move, as though it were made of jelly, refusing to obey his commands. He screwed up his eyes, summoning all his concentration and tried again. And failed a second time.

"Goddam you!" Cruse roared.

Calling up all his strength he threw the Storm-Trooper off him, and leapt to his feet, grabbing the zip-gun which had been knocked from his hand. He aimed it at the StormTrooper, and fired. There was a crackle of energy and the Trooper died instantly.

There wasn't a second to lose. Cruse fired on the approaching Troopers, and then turned and scaled the cliff. Kristas and Shari helped him over the edge.

Cruse glared at Kristas. "Why didn't you fire?" he barked. "You could have got me killed down there!"

Kristas shook his head and looked down at the zip-gun which he was still holding in his shaking hand. "I – I don't know," he said slowly. "I couldn't squeeze the trigger – there must be something wrong with it..."

Cruse grabbed the gun from Kristas and trained it on the StormTroopers down below who had just reached the foot of the cliff. It fired perfectly and he handed the gun back to Kristas, who looked bemused.

"I don't understand," Kristas said. "Why couldn't I fire it...?"

"I wonder," Cruse said, and eyed the younger man evilly.

"Let's get back to camp!" Shari urged them. "Those StormTroopers will be up the cliff in a second."

Cruse quickly reconnoitred the landscape: a

rubble-strewn expanse which seemed to stretch for miles. There were few landmarks or distinguishing features in the inky darkness that was falling fast: to all intents and purposes they were lost.

"Which way do we go?" he asked. "We don't even know how to get back to camp from here."

"Anywhere's better than being with those Troopers," Shari pointed out, and then felt Kristas grab her by the hand and lead her off to the north-west.

"Follow me," he said. "I know the way."

"And how the hell do you know that?" Cruse demanded.

"I *know*, that's all," said Kristas, and he and Shari started to move off. With a final parting shot at the StormTroopers who were preparing to scale the cliff, Cruse followed Kristas and Shari.

Several minutes later, the first of the StormTroopers reached the top of the cliff. He was a tall and wiry man named Commander Schreck, and was one of Donovan Trueheart's most trusted strong-arm men. He touched a control on the side of his helmet, and the visor in front of his eyes automatically adjusted itself to infra-red mode.

Schreck scanned the horizon, until he caught sight of Shari, Kristas and Cruse who were rapidly disappearing into the distance. He smiled, as the other Troopers joined him on the top of the cliff.

"Shall we go after them, Commander?" the first of them, Corporal Feder, asked.

"Five of you pursue them," Schreck said, and his voice was as dark and as oily as the polluted rivers on this God-forsaken planet. "But try not to be too persistent, will you, Feder? It is important that they reach their skimmer and escape..."

"Commander?" Feder was confused. "I thought we were to take them alive? I did not realize that they were to be allowed to escape as well..."

Schreck smiled, enjoying Feder's confusion. Schreck was a self-important man, who enjoyed being privy to secrets that his subordinates would never be trusted with, even if they could have understood them.

"You may –" here Schreck paused, considering his words – "you may damage their craft, Feder. One of the primary fuel tanks, I think. Leave them enough fuel for a flight of a hundred klicks."

"I do not understand, Commander," Feder persisted. "We ambush them, lose several of our men in the process, then let them escape – we may never find them again."

Schreck shook his head. "If your men do their task properly, Feder, there is only one place they can go to," he said, and pointed up at the streaks of light in the night sky. "The hunter-ships will 'attack' them, forcing them to travel in one direction only. And when they run out of fuel, we will know where they are and then the game can begin in earnest..."

"The game?" Feder was trying hard to understand.

"It is not for the likes of you to know the plans and machinations of your superiors," Schreck said, a threatening tone creeping into his voice.

"I have always been a loyal servant of the Trueheart," Feder claimed.

"Ah yes, the Trueheart, of course..." said Schreck, and the ends of his mouth twisted into a small ironical smile. "We are all loyal servants of the Trueheart..."

Schreck stood there for a moment, as if enjoying a private joke. Then he clapped his hands together, in a business-like fashion. "Arrange for a squad to pursue the outlaws," he ordered. "And tell me, Feder, how many men did we lose to that mercenary with the zip-gun?"

"Six," said Feder, and then added, almost admiringly: "He is a good fighter, Commander. Almost as good as us..."

"Six dead men?" said Schreck, and smiled. "Then we shall feast well this night!" He pointed back down to Doob's grave. "There is a small mammal buried there. Perhaps not the freshest of fare, but we must be grateful for small mercies!" He licked his lips. "After all, an army does march on its stomach, does it not?"

Fairest of Cities

Shari, Kristas and Cruse reached their skimmer – as planned by Commander Schreck – with minutes to spare. Cruse had no time to wonder why the StormTroopers were showing a suspicious inability to catch up with them, or even hit them, as he climbed into the cockpit of the small flying craft, revved the engines and booted up the on-board flight computer. Shari and Kristas clambered on board after him, and watched as his fingers flickered over the instruments. There was a whirring sound and the hatchway of the small craft closed.

"Where are we going?" Shari asked, as Cruse engaged the solar-powered engines, and she felt the skimmer prepare for horizontal take-off.

"Out of here, obviously," he replied through gritted teeth, without turning around to look at Shari. "Perhaps we should ask Kristas to show us the way. He got us back here, through unknown countryside. Like he's been here before..."

"What are you implying?" Kristas demanded.

Cruse grunted non-committally, and checked the read-outs from the computer. He engaged the power and the skimmer rose noisily from the ground, its engines blowing dirt and rubble in all directions. Down below, the StormTroopers, led by Feder, had caught up with them, and they started firing on the ship.

"Faster, Cruse!" Shari pleaded urgently. "Take us higher! They'll hit us!"

"Why should they start now?" Cruse said, affecting an air of nonchalance (although he also increased the power). "It's not our deaths that scum is after – is it?"

He glanced over at Kristas, and a dangerous look passed over the younger man's face, and he clenched his fist involuntarily. Kristas was about to say something when there was a massive explosion to the port-side of the skimmer, and the ship lurched sickeningly, throwing him and Shari against the cabin wall.

"We're hit!" Shari cried, as the skimmer began to spin out of control. In the pilot seat Cruse kept his nerve, glancing over at the computer display to assess the damage. He made a few adjustments to the controls, and the ship levelled off, and rose higher into the night sky. The viewer-screen showed the rapidly receding figures of the StormTroopers at ground level as they continued firing at the vessel, even as it sped out of range.

"Well done," Shari said, as Cruse slipped the ship on to automatic pilot, and examined the gridded screen of the flight path indicator.

"We're not out of danger yet," Cruse said, and pointed to several dots of light on the screen. They were rapidly converging on to their ship's flight path.

"What are they?" asked Kristas.

"Fairy lights," Cruse said. "What do you think they are? System hunter-ships!"

"Can we outrun them?" Shari asked.

Cruse nodded. "We're a small transport ship: we might be able to evade them." He glanced at an LED to the right of the cockpit controls, and cursed under his breath. "They've hit our main solar power stacks," he said, keeping his voice steady, despite the panic which he felt welling up inside him.

"What does that mean?" asked Kristas.

"We've enough power left for a journey of –" Cruse did a lightning-quick calculation – "about ninety-six klicks."

"Are you sure?"

"Fly ninety-seven klicks, and you'll see I'm right when we crash!" Cruse retorted, and returned to the flight path indicator. "Now be quiet and let me think! You've caused enough trouble already!"

That was too much for Kristas to take. He reached

out and grabbed Cruse's shoulder, making him turn around to look at him. "I've had enough of your snide comments," he snarled. "Why don't you start saying what you mean?"

Cruse glowered at the younger man. "OK, I will," he said. "It was you who insisted that we bury Doob at nightfall in an open place. Just when those StormTroopers were prowling around."

"What the System are you trying to say?" Kristas asked, scarcely able to believe what he was hearing. "You're surely not trying to say that I knew we were going to be attacked?"

"That's crazy," Shari agreed. "You're not suggesting that Kristas led us into some sort of ambush?"

"Did I say that?" Cruse grunted, and nodded over at Kristas before addressing Shari. "I've been watching him all day," he said. "He's been edgy and nervous, on tenterhooks, like a cat before a big storm. Like he's been expecting something to happen..."

"Those StormTroopers were firing at me as well, in case you hadn't noticed!" Kristas pointed out sarcastically. "And it might also have escaped your notice that it was me who got us back to the skimmer!"

"Yeah," Cruse said begrudgingly. "By a route we've never used, across country we've never crossed before. Or at least Shari and I haven't. You seemed to know every inch of the way..."

"Will you two cut it out!" Shari shouted, coming

between the two men. "You can sort out your stupid differences later! For the moment let's concentrate on escaping those hunter-ships." She pointed to the screen: the blips of light were closing in on them.

"Shari's right," Kristas said, and struggled to control his temper. "Can we lose them, with the power reserves we've got left?"

Cruse peered at the screen, and nodded. "If we keep to a low flight path, and head north, we might just lose them up in the Wastes. Only a fool would want to follow us in there."

Shari's face fell, and she felt her throat tighten with apprehension. She had heard stories of the Wastes before and of the creatures which dwelt there. "We wouldn't survive for long there; pollution's even worse the more inland you get,' she said, but Cruse just raised his eyes heavenwards and sighed.

"You got any better ideas?" he asked. "With our limited power supplies that's the only chance we have."

Shari bowed her head. "I suppose you know best," she said meekly. After three years of knowing him, Cruse could still make her feel like a naïve little kid.

"I'm gratified to hear it," Cruse said, and returned to the flight controls. Shari walked to the rear of the cabin where Kristas was sitting on one of the pull-down seats which lined the wall.

"Are you OK?" she asked, and Kristas nodded. "I'm sure he didn't mean what he said. It's just that when things get tough he has to have someone to blame, someone to lash out at. When he's faced with something he can't understand his only option is to fight it. He's always been like that. And if he didn't trust you we wouldn't have been together, all three of us, for the past three years."

Kristas nodded, knowing in his heart of hearts that Shari was right. He raised a hand to his forehead and rubbed it gently. "All he's done is succeed in giving me another headache," he said ruefully.

"You're sure you're not sickening for something?" Shari asked and regretted the words as soon as she had said them. They had each remained reasonably healthy during their stay on the polluted Earth, apart from an initial bout of sunstroke. Their skin had taken time adapting to the sun's ultra-violet light, which was no longer filtered through an ozone layer as strong as it had been years ago. Yet they all knew that life-threatening disease could strike swiftly, as it had with Doob, airborne plagues from which even their regular use of oxy-masks couldn't protect them. Kristas's recurring headaches could be just a result of stress, Shari reasoned; they could also be the presager of something much more deadly.

Kristas looked at the blips of light on the flight-path indicator, and changed the subject. "Why aren't they catching up with us?" he asked Shari.

"Cruse is a good pilot," Shari said. "If anyone can outmanoeuvre them then he can."

"I know. . . But it's as if they don't *want* to catch us," he said. "They're like dogs herding sheep, making them go where they want them to go. . ."

"That's silly," Shari said. "Why ever would they want to spare our lives? We're renegades, refugees from the System. . . What possible use could any of us be to them?"

Twenty-five million klicks above the Earth, sitting in his sumptuous private chambers, the Child Roland allowed himself the briefest of smiles. On the small desktop smart-box before him, he tracked the flight of the hunter-ships as they searched out Shari and their friends. Commander Schreck had performed his side of the bargain perfectly.

The Commander was a good soldier, the Child Roland realized, so good, in fact, that he thought he would allow him to live just a little longer. He would have to die in the end, of course; he was merely a hireling, a tool, not one of the Chosen, and inferior beings such as he could never be trusted for long. They always demanded more favours, more credits, more food, and that would never do.

The door to his office swished open, and the Child Roland hurriedly shut down his computer, and then turned around. When he recognized his visitor, he broke into a smile which made his youthful features appear even more juvenile.

"Dera," he said, and strode forwards to embrace

the attractive young red-headed woman standing in the doorway. "It's wonderful to see you again."

Dera kissed the Child Roland on the lips, and then walked over to the drinks cabinet. She poured herself a glass of the wine which Donovan Trueheart had presented to Roland. She offered one to Roland but he declined, as she knew he would.

"You have been neglecting me, Roland," she reproved and gave a little-girl moue of displeasure, even though she was several years older than Roland.

"I know," Roland admitted and put an arm around her waist. "But what can I do? The Trueheart needs me more every day: it's my mission to tell the people just how much he loves them, and that he wants nothing more than their continued good fortune."

"The Trueheart," Dera said, with something which sounded dangerously like scorn. "Sometimes I think that you love him more than you love me. You certainly spend most of your time with him!"

"Now, you know that's not true," Roland said, and fixed her with those dark, boyish eyes which he knew could drive any woman wild. "Didn't I take you to the Pleasure Grounds of Titan only the other week? And who was it who bought you that fur, specially skinned from one of our genetically-augmented minks?"

Dera nodded her head. "I know, and I'm grateful for that," she said sincerely. "But surely you can delegate some of your duties to others? What can be so important that it keeps you away from me for such long periods of time?"

"Let's not talk about such things now," Roland said.

"I've heard strange stories recently, Roland," Dera began.

The Child Roland took his arm away from Dera's waist and frowned. "Stories? What sort of stories?"

Dera hesitated, as though she was unsure how much she could say to Roland, and then continued: "Just little rumours. That there's unrest down on TerraNova, that some people don't believe that the Trueheart loves them as much as he says he does."

"Now, you know that's ridiculous," the Child Roland said in a gently reproving voice. "The Trueheart regards us all as his children, especially as he has not been blessed by offspring himself. Who has been telling you these silly stories?"

"Karla and Alana," Dera said, referring to two of her closest friends. "They say that some parts of the System may soon be facing famine, and that it's all the Trueheart's fault..."

Roland tut-tutted, like a disapproving parent gently upbraiding a child. "What nonsense your friends talk!" he said lightly, as though he was unconcerned by the news. "I shall have to have a word with them..."

For a second Dera panicked. "I didn't mean to get

them into any sort of trouble, Roland," she said hurriedly, but he hushed her.

"*The System provides and we are content,*" he said, repeating the article of faith which every child had to learn in the schoolroom. "You do believe me, don't you, Dera?"

Dera nodded, grateful that she hadn't angered the man she loved above all else. "Of course," she said. "They're just silly rumours, like those tales about old Earth. . ."

Roland smiled at her. "I'm glad you see the truth at last," he breathed, and walked towards the door. "I have to see the Trueheart now –"

"But Roland –"

Roland laughed, and kissed her affectionately on the cheek. "Only for an hour or so," he said. "And then I'm at your disposal for the rest of the evening! And Dera –"

"Yes?"

"I do love you."

"And I love you too, Roland," Dera smiled and gave her lover a little wave as he walked out of his private chambers and into the corridor beyond.

As soon as the door closed shut behind him, the Child Roland turned to the armed security guard who was permanently stationed outside his quarters.

"Kill her," he said, and glanced back towards the room in which Dera was waiting. "And her two friends, Karla and Alana, as well. They have heard too much, said far more than they should have. Make it look like an accident, of course."

The guard nodded, and moved towards the door.

"And one more thing as well," said the Child Roland. "Destroy her apartments too – who knows what subversive literature the traitress may have lying around there? But spare her mink coat – I paid good credits for that. . ."

Ninety-six klicks inland lay the Waste: a blighted and toxic desert of shattered buildings and cratered earth on the shores of a river which ran black and fetid down to the sea. The Waste, so people said, had been a major industrial and political centre on old Earth, before humans had polluted their environment so much that their only hope of survival was to colonize another world, in this case the recently terraformed planet Mars, renamed TerraNova by the all-powerful System.

Now the Waste remained, shrouded in what seemed to be an eternal fog, a silent memorial to man's destruction of his own planet.

It was dawn when Cruse's battered and damaged skimmer managed a shaky touchdown on the banks of the river, and in the rusty-coloured sky the sun was rising, bringing with it an increase in temperature from the night's sub-zero coldness.

Even so, Shari still hugged herself for warmth as she and Kristas stumbled out of the craft, leaving Cruse to see what repairs he could make to the ship's solar stacks. Their breath hung in clouds before their faces as they walked down to the river.

"It's horrible," she said, and coughed. The fog she was breathing in had an acidic tang to it: she wouldn't be surprised to discover that continued exposure to it would burn out her lungs. "It's even worse than the coast."

Kristas peered through the fog at the skeletal shapes of buildings long deserted; most of them were now nothing more than piles of rubble, but some still stood proud and defiant on the river bank. A half-shattered tower still rose majestically to the skies, even though the buildings adjacent to it were little more than piles of broken bricks and stones, and twisted and rusted iron girders. Nearby he could just make out the silhouette of another building – a massive edifice of granite and shattered windows, looking like a ruined ancient fortress.

"Surely nothing can live here?" he said. He crouched down and scooped up a handful of earth: it was black and dry and he let it skitter between his fingers and fall down to the ground. "The whole place is dead."

Shari walked up to the nearest fallen stone: it was covered with a grey ash. "Radioactive fallout," she muttered darkly.

Kristas stood up and even in the half-light of early

dawn – did it ever get any lighter? – Shari could see the panic in his eyes.

"Fallout?' he asked urgently, but Shari smiled and put a reassuring hand on his shoulder. He brushed it off awkwardly.

"Relax, we're in no danger," she said. "The fallout was years ago. Remember the Great Colonial War?"

Kristas shrugged. "I studied languages at the Academy, not history," he reminded her.

"It was a dispute between two great colonies – Wessex, and the Kentish Moot." Kristas looked blankly at her, and Shari continued, "Wessex was a republic somewhere to the west of here, I guess. The Kentish Moot used to cover the whole south-east connurbation of this island. This was just before everything was taken over and administered by the System. No one's quite sure why they fell out – it's possible that it was the result of a rogue computer virus introduced by a third power."

"That was always a problem with smart-boxes before the invention of bio-cybernetics and the introduction of direct brain-to-computer link-ups," Kristas remarked. "The systems were much too easy to hack into."

"Anyway, the war went on for thirty minutes," Shari said, almost casually as though she was a teacher, addressing her students in one of the lecture halls of the Academy.

Kristas whistled. "Thirty minutes? That long?"

52

Shari nodded. "The Kentish Moot lost," she continued. "Wessex exploded a huge neutron bomb over the entire area. Trouble was, it wiped out most of Wessex as well. But that was well over a thousand years ago — whatever radioactive fallout there was would have ceased to be harmful now." She trailed her hand through the ash. "At least I think so... Still, the sooner we're out of here the better..."

"A neutron bomb," Kristas said, half to himself. "It wipes out all life, but leaves the buildings more or less intact..."

"That's right," Shari said. "But what's the point of leaving buildings standing when there's no one around to live in them?"

"How many people died in the War?"

"Hard to tell — you know how the System files never agree with each other," Shari said in an off-hand manner. "But I'd guess about thirty-five million — give or take a million."

Kristas was silent for a moment, and turned away from Shari to look at the fortress-like building by the tower; the reddish rays of the rising sun reflected off the shattered glass of one of its windows, comforting Kristas in a strange way.

"Thirty-five million people," he repeated, and Shari had the weirdest feeling that he was not addressing her, but the building itself. "Babies who opened their eyes one morning, only to feel them melted away by unimaginable heat. Lovers who reached out to each other, only to feel their flesh peeling away at the touch... How could anyone order the mass annihilation of thirty-five million innocent people?"

Shari looked strangely at Kristas; she had never heard him speak this way before. "It was war, Kristas," she said softly. "It was one of the reasons the System was founded – so that mankind would never go to war with each other again. And it happened a long time ago."

"That doesn't make it any better," he said, still not looking at her. "And there were still wars after that..."

"It was war, Kristas," she repeated, and then added, "These things happen..."

Kristas spun round. "How can you be so unfeeling?" he snapped at her. "You're getting as hard and as cynical as Cruse! Thirty-five million people died here and you make it sound as though that's nothing!"

Shari was shocked by Kristas's sudden change of mood. "You know I don't treat death lightly – I hate it," she defended herself. "*But it was over a thousand years ago!*"

"It might as well have been yesterday," he said, calmer now. He ran his hand through the ash which covered a nearby granite block. "This ash could be all that remains of the people who lived here." He turned back to Shari, and she could see a tortured and tormented look in his eyes. "I can hear them, Shari, hear their screams in that final second when they realized what was happening and felt the heat of a thousand suns blazing through their bodies..."

Shari came forward and put an arm around Kristas. "You've changed, Kristas," she said softly. "You were always sensitive, always caring, but I've never seen you like this before."

"You think I should be like Cruse, then?" The question was asked almost grudgingly. "I can skin a chicken, start a fire with a pair of dried-out twigs, bind a wound with a poultice. I can even scale a cliff if I want to..."

But you can't fire a zip-gun, can you? At least not to save Cruse, Shari thought.

"Should I also try to be as callous and as heartless as he is?"

"He's not!" Shari said, rising immediately to her friend's defence. "He's risked his life for us more than once, and you know it! If he was so heartless, why would he spend his time rescuing mutants from the System? And he loved Marla once – I think he always will..."

"And you've changed too, Shari," Kristas said, in a recriminating fashion. "You're harder, tougher, more bitter. You spend too much time with Cruse..."

Shari took her arm away from Kristas. There was an outraged expression on her face. "For System's sake!" she said, reverting in her anger to the phrases of their old life. "You're my friend, Kristas, not my jealous boyfriend! And Cruse isn't my boyfriend either, for that matter! What gives you the right to tell me how and with whom I should spend my time!"

"We used to be so good together, Shari," Kristas said nostalgically. "Kristas and Shari — two best friends who escaped the System to live out life amongst the stars."

"We couldn't have done it without Cruse," Shari pointed out angrily. "And since we're stranded here there are now three of us and not two, and you're going to have to like it or lump it! Or go off to wherever it is you go when you vanish for hours at a time. Maybe Cruse is right. Maybe you are up to something you don't want us to know about!"

Shari regretted her words instantly and there was a long pause as the two friends stared accusingly at each other. Finally it was Shari who broke the silence. "I'm sorry, Kristas," she said, and meant it. "You've got a perfect right to your privacy if you want it. It's just this planet — this constant living on the edge, hiding from the System, like hunted prey — it's winding us all up..."

"Maybe I'm sorry too," Kristas said, although not without a self-indulgent sulk. "And I'll try to get on better with Cruse."

"We are all in this mess together, you know," Shari said, and smiled when Kristas nodded his head in agreement. "We have to stick together. No matter what our differences are, we're all the same."

Kristas turned away for a moment. *You're right, Shari*, he said to himself. *We are all the same. But then why do I feel so different? Why do I see things, hear voices, that you and Cruse don't...*

He turned back to Shari. "This place stinks of death," he said. "Nothing must have lived here for hundreds of years. Even the ash has remained."

"There's no wind to disturb it," Shari said. "But I'm not so sure about nothing living here."

Kristas arched an eyebrow. "What d'you mean?" he asked.

"I've heard rumours about this place from the mutants we've helped," she said. "They talk of people who live amongst the rubble of the old cities. Descendants, they say, of those people who survived the neutron bomb, and who elected to remain on the Earth when the rest of the planet's surviving population was moved to Mars. The Charred People, they call them..."

"That's impossible," Kristas argued. "No one could have survived the blast."

Shari was non-committal: in truth she did not know what to think. "Maybe they survived in bomb shelters?" she supposed. "Or some freak geographical feature of meteorological activity protected them from the fallout?"

"If they did survive, what would their descendants

look like?" Kristas asked. "The mutants we help aren't really mutants – they've been genetically altered by the System. What would people who had to mutate naturally – to survive in this hell-hole – look like?" He shivered.

"Are you cold?" Shari asked. *Is it a fever?* were the words which ran through her mind, words which she tried to block out.

Kristas shook his head, and looked warily around. "It felt as if someone had just walked over my grave," he said. "Don't you get the feeling that we're not alone here?"

Shari frowned. Kristas had always had a vivid imagination, and she should have known better than to have told him about the Charred People. Kristas had been plagued by bad dreams lately, she knew; she didn't want to be responsible for any more of his nightmares.

"Let's get back to Cruse," she suggested and gazed through the fog at the sleek silhouette of the skimmer. The other member of their party was working on the outside of the craft now, trying to repair the damage caused by the System Troopers. She waved at him, but either he didn't see her through the fog, or he chose to ignore her.

Shrugging her shoulders, Shari started to move up the river bank and towards Cruse. Kristas followed, his eyes darting this way and that, as if looking for something. When he caught up with Shari, he pointed out the building by the tower.

"It's beautiful," he said.

Shari stopped for a moment to look at the building through the fog. "It's not half as beautiful as Saint Paul's," she said, and in answer to Kristas's blank look, added helpfully, "It was an ancient cathedral, in a city called London. They razed it to the ground centuries ago to make way for a spaceport... You do know what a cathedral is, don't you?"

Kristas, who seemed to have regained some of his former good humour, cheerfully admitted that he didn't.

"They were huge places of worship," Shari explained. "Where people came together to praise God."

"God?"

"Never mind."

They had nearly reached Cruse now, and Shari started to run up towards him. And stopped. And grabbed hold of Kristas with such an urgency that her fingernails dug deep into his flesh.

Something had come between them and Cruse. It was a wolf, but a wolf the like of which neither of them had ever seen before. The creature was at least one-and-a-half metres high, and twice that length from the tip of its tail to its quivering snout. Cold, baleful eyes glared at them, and it opened its mouth, to display razor-sharp teeth through which globs of saliva dripped on to the dry earth. It growled at them threateningly, its long pointed ears twitching, as it reared on its haunches, ready to pounce.

"Don't take your eyes off it," Cruse's voice called out steadily from the side of the skimmer. "Walk slowly away from it. . ."

Shari and Kristas did as they were told, while all the while the wolf fixed them with its awful stare. It licked its lips, anticipating the taste of this fresh new meat which had so conveniently presented itself, and it growled again.

Something in Shari seemed to snap, and she turned her face away from the predator, and up the hill towards Cruse. The wolf howled, and leapt on her, bringing her down to the ground with a bone-jarring *crunch*! Shari screamed and attempted to push the beast off her, but the animal was too strong, and it was all she could do to stop it ripping at her neck.

"Cruse, do something!" she cried out, and she was dimly aware of Cruse racing down from the skimmer towards her.

And then there was what seemed to Shari to be a massive, deafening explosion, and the wolf jerked, stiffened, and fell back from her. Shari felt something wet and sticky on the front of her tunic, and for one horrifying moment thought that the blast from the zip-gun had hit her in the chest. Then she realized that the blood had come from the wolf, which was lying by her side now, a steaming carcass of flesh and blood.

Cruse knelt down by her side, and raised her head so that he could see her face; his own was racked with worry.

"You OK?" he asked.

Shari nodded. "Thank you, Cruse," she said, and was surprised when the young mercenary shook his head.

"Don't thank me," he said, and nodded over to Kristas, who was standing a little way off, his zip-gun in his hand. "It was Kristas who shot the wolf, not me. I was too far away: if I'd've fired there was a chance that I would have hit you by accident."

Shari sat up, and looked at Kristas. "Thank you, Kristas..." she said.

Kristas looked at the gun, and then at the steaming carcass of the wolf. "Is it dead?" he asked, bemused.

"Of course it's dead!" Cruse sneered. "Nothing could stand a blast like that from such close quarters. Seems that you're a fine shot when it comes to saving Shari – but not so good when it's my life that's on the line!"

Shari glared at Cruse; they were in enough trouble already – did he really have to make things worse? And yet he did have a point: Kristas had been unable to use the zip-gun when Cruse was being attacked by one of the StormTroopers but had proved himself a crack shot just now. Surely Kristas hadn't wanted Cruse killed before?

Suddenly Shari didn't know what to think, as she looked over at Kristas who was shaking his head repeatedly and saying over and over, "I didn't mean to kill it, I didn't mean to kill it. . ."

Cruse helped Shari to her feet, and she staggered over to look at the body of the animal which had tried to kill her. Its snout was longer and thinner than the pictures of wolves she had seen on holo-disks back at the Academy, and its teeth were razor-sharp.

"What is it?" she asked Cruse, and tried hard not to gag on the stench which was already rising from the creature's carcass. "A lupe?"

Cruse shook his head. "Lupes are an artificially engineered species, a cross between lions and wolves," he said. "You won't find them on Earth. Earth is the dumping ground for the System's botched experiments, but the lupe is regarded as one of its successes – brutal, cleanly efficient killers, and fiercely loyal to their masters. No wonder Trueheart is so fond of them."

"Not Trueheart, but *the* Trueheart," Kristas said. "He likes to be called the Trueheart these days. . ."

Shari and Cruse ignored the comment, and Shari continued to look at the wolf. "If it's a wolf then it's unlike any I've seen before," she said. "Look at the snout for one thing. And it's much bigger than a normal wolf. And wolves usually hunt in packs – but this one is obviously a loner."

"They must have evolved then," Kristas said, and all eyes turned to him. "Adapted themselves to changing environmental circumstances."

"He's right," said Cruse. "The survival of the fittest. Every species from the tiniest plant right up to *homo sapiens* is subject to the laws of evolution, developing whatever talents it needs to survive. But there's one thing that worries me . . ."

"Which is?" asked Shari.

"This wolf is well-fed," he said. "Almost over-weight. If he'd have been quicker and leaner, Shari, you wouldn't have stood a chance against him; he'd have torn out your throat before you'd even known what was happening."

"So why does that worry you?" This was from Kristas. "The fatter he is the more meat we'll have to eat."

"I don't think I want to eat anything from this place," Shari said. "Surely everything's poisoned . . ."

"He didn't get this fat through burrowing for the odd seed in the ground with that specially thin snout of his, did he?" Cruse asked. "This beauty's feasted off living flesh. And that means only one thing – humans. Somewhere in this hell-pit there are other people!"

"The Charred People," said Kristas, and trembled. "I knew someone was watching us!"

"Then whoever else is here can help us repair our skimmer," Shari said.

Cruse nodded grimly, "Maybe – if they have the technology, which I very much doubt," he muttered. "Of course, they could see us as tonight's supper!"

Muhajji

The biped peered intently through the mists, watching Shari, Cruse and Kristas as they busied themselves around their skimmer. His eyes were large and grey, out of all proportion to his tiny wizened head, and they protruded out of withered sockets. He licked his lips with a leathery tongue; there was plenty of meat on these three newcomers, and it was a long time since he had fed on such succulent-looking flesh.

It took all his willpower and self-control for the creature not to leap out of the shadows and attack them. But he had seen what Kristas had done with the zip-gun, killing the wolf, just as easily as the wolves killed the Charred People. He would be wise to be wary of that one: there was something strange about that blond-haired boy, he was sure. He frowned, as a long-forgotten memory tried to resurface in his mind. For some reason he knew the boy was important, but when he tried to remember just *why* the sudden pain in his head was so great that he chose not to pursue the matter.

For the moment, therefore, the creature contented itself by watching, and listening with its ears, pointed and sharp, like a dog's, twitching, catching the slightest whisper, the faintest footfall. It knew what it had to do, had indeed been waiting for this moment for a long time now, ever since it had first become aware of the presence of the three rebels in a dream. That was why he had been sent here, he guessed, that was why he had been waiting these long years.

"There's nothing I can do,' he heard Cruse say, as the lanky mercenary turned away from the skimmer, and slapped his hands together, to dust off the dirt and the grease.

"What d'you mean?" asked Kristas.

"Exactly what I said," Cruse muttered darkly. "The skimmer's well and truly wasted. Those fuel panels won't get us very far–" he looked off, through the mist and over the rubble-strewn horizon, as though trying to gauge a distance – "twenty-odd klicks, if we're lucky, and then –" He slapped a fist into the palm of another hand, imitating the motion of a crashing spacecraft.

"You mean, we're stranded here?" asked Shari in disbelief. She looked around her nervously. Kristas was right – it did feel as though someone was watching them.

Cruse nodded. "There's no point wasting our time out here," he said, practically, and glanced down at the carcass of the wolf. "We need to take cover – who knows how many of those wolves are about, all begging for a meal. First thing, we find a place of safety – then we worry about what we're going to do."

Kristas looked at the building by the tower. "Sanctuary," he muttered.

Cruse shrugged. "Call it what you like, it's as good a place as any," he said. He started to trudge up the small hill towards the building; Shari and Kristas followed, and then, in turn, were followed by the creature which had been hiding in the mists, watching them.

Within minutes they had reached the building, and were standing before an archway made of heavy and weathered stone, whose elaborate carvings had long been shot off by the blast from the bombs. Two heavy wooden doors, scorched and blackened, but still serviceable, hung off their rusted hinges.

Cruse pushed the doors open and the three of them walked through the arch and into the interior of the building. Unknown to them, and as soundlessly as thought, the creature padded after them.

"It's beautiful," said Shari, as she stared up at the vaulted ceiling, open to the sky, and through which the sun was shining weakly. Huge castellated pillars towered to the heavens, dwarfing the three new-comers; other pillars had fallen to the ground, where they lay shattered and broken.

At the far end of the chamber was a large arched window, made of thousands upon thousands of tiny panels of differently-coloured glass; the sun's light glittered and gleamed through them, swathing the rubble and detritus-strewn floor in a rainbow blanket of colours.

"What is it?" asked Kristas, scarcely able to believe the sheer enormity of the place. And there was something else too: even in all its destruction, there was a strange sort of serenity here, in total contrast to the ash and slag and the toxic mists which sur-rounded it. It was as if all the wars of the past few centuries had never happened, as if all those inno-cent lives from Wessex and the Kentish Moot had been spared, and as if the cruel and harsh System itself had never come into being as a direct result of those wars.

"A graveyard, nothing else," laughed Cruse and kicked his way through the rubble to a huge stone box, its lid lying by its side. He looked over the rim at the box's contents: a human skeleton.

"A stone coffin?" asked Shari, and grimaced when she saw the skeleton. "What's it doing here?"

Cruse reached down to the skeleton and it crumbled at his touch, turning into greyish dust. *As grey as the rest of this damned planet*, he thought.

"It's not the only one," he said, and gestured at several other stone sarcophagi, lined up along the wall. He was about to go over to examine them more closely, when Shari called him back. She was kneeling down at the upturned lid of the coffin.

"There's something written on it," she said, and frowned as she tried to make out the unfamiliar letters etched into the stone. "*Hic... iacet... Guillamus Quintus... senator Europi et rex Anglorum...*" She stood up. The words meant nothing to her.

"I know what they mean," Kristas said, excitedly. "Remember – I studied languages at the Academy back home on Pasiphae. It's Latin, the old language of the Romans!" He peered down at the words inscribed in the stone, and translated: "Here lies William the Fifth, Senator of Europe, and King of the English..." He turned to the others: "William the Fifth? Who was he?"

Now it was Shari's turn to be excited. "The last King of England, before it was broken up into regional republics!" She looked around her. "And now I know where we are – Westminster Abbey!"

Even Cruse allowed himself to be impressed. "So we're in London," he realized. "Or rather, what's left of it..."

"Once the greatest city in the world," Kristas remembered from the boring history lessons he had been forced to attend as a young child. "And now look at it – a wasteland."

Cruse slapped Kristas on the back. "It's evolved, that's what it's done, dreamer!" he joked darkly. "Adapted to changing environmental circumstances like a few thousand neutron bombs, and kilos of poisonous waste discharged into the atmosphere!"

"That's not funny, Cruse," Shari reproved him, and made her way further into the Abbey. A featureless stone slab dominated the space. "This must be where they held their services, and worshipped God..." she said, and tried to ignore Cruse's disbelieving guffaw. She turned around and looked at Kristas.

"Sanctuary, you called it. You knew, didn't you? In the ancient times, churches and cathedrals offered sanctuary to people in trouble."

Kristas shook his head. "I didn't know, Shari, I promise you," he said, and the tone of his voice proved that he was just as confused as she was. "All I knew was that we would be safe here. I didn't even know what the abbey looked like until a few minutes ago."

While Shari and Kristas were talking, Cruse was wandering around the main part of the Abbey, looking for somewhere in which they could shelter. He finally found a small side chapel whose roof had not caved in, and whose two doors, on opposite walls, offered them a choice of escape routes should they be attacked by the wolves – or whatever lay out there in the mist and fog.

He returned to them, and pointed out the chapel, before turning to his companions. "Shari, you're the history major," he said, suddenly all brusque and business-like. "What are the chances of finding some technical equipment in this fetid dungheap of a city?"

Shari frowned and tried to remember her ancient history lessons. "When the Earth was evacuated, London was turned into a huge factory site to build and service the spacecraft headed for Mars," she said. "I suppose some of those buildings may still be standing, but there's no guarantee that the System would have left any equipment or power stacks behind."

Cruse shook his head. "Maybe not now, with the System on the point of starvation, and its mineral reserves running out," he said. "But in the old days, when they were so confident that their glorious empire would last a thousand years –'

"It has lasted a thousand years," Kristas pointed out. Cruse glared at him and the younger man shrugged and moved away.

"In the old days they'd just abandon equipment when they no longer had a need for it," he continued. "They had no plans to return to Earth anyway – so why not use it as their interplanetary dustbin?"

"That still doesn't mean that any power stacks

would remain serviceable after such a long time," Shari pointed out.

"It's the only hope we've got," Cruse said. "Apart from sub-tachyon power, solar and crystal technology hasn't changed much over the centuries. That's why the System's scientists started exploring sub-light power sources: technologically speaking, Earth had reached a cul-de-sac."

Shari shrugged: it was a slim hope, but, as Cruse had said, it was the only hope they had."

"Can you remember where those sites were based?" Cruse asked her.

"To the south of here," Shari recalled. "Across the Thames."

"The what?"

"The river," she explained, and smiled indulgently at Cruse.

"We can forget about that then," Cruse said. "That river's poisonous. Even if we could build a raft, there's probably enough acid in the waters to eat right through it before we're even halfway across!"

"There used to be bridges across the Thames," Shari remembered. "But I don't recall seeing any when we landed here."

"Not that you can see much in the damn fog," Cruse said. "D'you think it ever clears?"

"Probably not," Shari said gloomily. "But we have to get out of here, Cruse. Can't we use the skimmer?

You said yourself it can still take us about twenty klicks."

Cruse shook his head. "I don't want to use it if we can at all help it," he said firmly. "Those System hunters might still be after us..." He frowned, and rubbed his chin thoughtfully. "They could have shot us down any time," he realized, "but they didn't..."

"That's because you're such a good pilot," Shari said, truthfully. "One of the best."

"I'm not *that* good," he said. "It was almost like they wanted us to get away ... or as if we were carrying some sort of valuable cargo..."

"Both of you, come over here!"

Shari and Cruse turned around, and saw Kristas. He was about four metres away from them, and kneeling on the ground, looking at something in the rubble. They walked over to him; he looked up at them and there was an enormous grin on his face.

"Isn't it great?" he said, and plucked something from the ground. He handed it to Shari.

"A daisy?' Shari said, wondering what all the fuss was about. There had been no end of daisies back home on Pasiphae.

"That's right," Kristas said; he could hardly contain the joy in his voice. He nodded down to the ground where a large patch of the tiny white flowers were growing in the cracks in the abbey floor.

Cruse took the flower from Shari, and examined it. It was slightly different from the daisies he had seen before: this one, for instance, was about twice the normal size, and its petals were streaked with lines of grey. "So it's a daisy," he shrugged. "So what?"

Kristas raised his eyes heavenwards in a gesture of exasperation. "So it proves that the ground might not be quite as barren as we thought. If daisies can grow here, who knows what else might?"

"Like toadstools," said Shari, as she noticed a small clump of fungus growing along the bottom of the wall of one of the side-chapels.

"Remember what I told you, Shari," Kristas said, as he stood up to join her. "Nature always wins through in the end – despite all that we do to it, despite the toxins we pour into its waters, despite the System, she always gets the upper hand."

"Those toadstools are probably just as poisonous," Cruse said gloomily, as he watched Shari bend down and pick one up.

And then the earth shook – a gentle tremor at first, but one which quickly grew into a thunderous rumble as the ground beneath Shari, Cruse and Kristas's feet buckled and bent. Shari lost her balance and fell over, and Cruse and Kristas grabbed hold of each other to keep upright. From far off came the sound of falling masonry, and shattering glass.

And then it was over, and the interior of Westminster Abbey was as quiet and as serene as it had always been. Cruse and Kristas awkwardly released themselves from each other's arms, and Cruse went

74

over to help Shari to her feet. She was still holding the toadstool she had picked, and she laughed nervously.

"I only pulled out one toadstool," she joked. "There was no need for the ground to get so upset."

"What *was* that?" asked Kristas, and looked around. They seemed to be safe, although some suspicious-looking fissures had appeared on the walls. "An earthquake?"

"Don't be an idiot," Cruse said. "There are no earthquakes in London!"

"Or at least there weren't," Shari pointed out. "The System has upset the atmosphere; who knows what else it might have done... Cruse, what are you doing?"

Cruse had fallen to his knees and was feeling the ground beneath their feet. He took Shari's hand and pressed it to the ground as well.

"It's warm!" she said, although the temperature of the earth was getting colder by the second. "But that doesn't make sense."

"A lot of things around here don't make sense," Cruse told her. "Thick fogs that don't lift, well-fed wolves that hunt alone, rivers pumped with toxins, and earthquakes in the middle of London. What do you think, Kristas? – Kristas?" Cruse turned around but Kristas was nowhere to be seen. "Damn him!" he cursed. "Where's he got to now?"

"We must find him!" Shari said.

"And walk into a trap?' Cruse sneered.

"What do you mean?"

"We're still alive when the System could have easily shot us out of the sky, aren't we?" Cruse said.

"Meaning?" Shari stared at Cruse, daring him to give voice to his suspicions.

Cruse averted his gaze, so as not to look at Shari. The truth – a truth he would die rather than admit – was that he trusted Kristas, despite their differences of opinion. If it had been any one other than Kristas, he would have told Shari that he suspected him of being in league with the enemy. But Kristas had never shown anything but loyalty to him and Shari, and yet his headaches, his mysterious disappearances, his strange hunches which always proved to be correct, they worried Cruse. For ten long years he had trusted no one since Marla, and then Shari and Kristas had come along and he had thought that, in them, he could recover the friendship he had once had with Marla and their companions at the Academy. Was he to be betrayed again?

"I know what you're trying to say," Shari said. "But we've all of us been through a lot together – why would Kristas betray us to the System?"

"Never trust anyone, Shari," Cruse stated flatly, hoping that she wouldn't recognize the lie in his eyes.

"You should trust me," said a cracked voice from the shadows.

Cruse whipped out his zip-gun and aimed it in the direction of the voice. Shari raised a hand to check him: they had no idea whether the person hiding in the shadows was friend or foe.

"Kristas was right!" Shari realized. "Someone was following us! But how could he have known?"

"Get out of the shadows," Cruse snarled at the figure in the blackness. "To where I can see you."

"So that you can shoot me dead?" the voice asked sarcastically.

"He won't shoot you," Shari reassured the figure. "You have my word."

"Then I choose to trust you," came the voice, and Cruse and Shari watched as the figure shambled out of the shadows, and into the light.

Shari found herself turning away in distaste when she saw the skull-like head, the flesh wasted and stretched taut over sharp cheekbones, the thin crop of ginger hair, and the eyes, red and raw-ringed, flickering about nervously. A gob of saliva dribbled down the creature's chin. His body, clothed in dirty rags, was thin and wiry, but still possessed great power, although he dragged one foot behind him, as though he was suffering from some long-standing injury.

She heard Cruse whisper softly in her ear, urging her to turn back and look at the stranger. She did so, noticing that although Cruse seemed unthreatened by the newcomer, he still kept his zip-gun trained on him.

"Who are you?" Cruse demanded.

"I am Muhajji," the stranger answered.

"Are you one of the – one of the Charred People?" Shari asked, and Muhajji shook his head.

"You're a mutant then," Cruse said gently. For all his gruffness, the mercenary felt genuine pity for all the victims of the System's genetic experiments.

"Perhaps," said Muhajji.

"What d'you mean, 'perhaps'?" Cruse's voice regained its characteristic brusqueness.

"I cannot remember," Muhajji admitted. "All I can recall is being found two years ago, by the shores of the poisoned river. Where I had been before is a blank. . ."

"I'm sorry," Shari said, and moved forward and sympathetically touched the man on the arm. His skin was burnt and blistered.

Cruse strode up to Muhajji; he had lowered his gun, but had not yet returned it to its holster. "You've been following us," he said. "Why?"

"I need your help," Muhajji said, and before he could explain further, Cruse snapped, "What's in it for us?"

"Your ship is damaged," Muhajji said.

"It might be," Cruse said, unwilling to give too much away.

"Your ship is damaged," Muhajji repeated. "Among my people – or rather the ones who found me two years ago – are many scientists. They can help repair your skimmer, give you your freedom again. If you stay here the System will surely track you down."

Cruse regarded Muhajji suspiciously. "And why should I believe you?" he asked.

"Trust?" suggested Muhajji, and Shari felt Cruse bristle.

"Your people," Shari said, "they're the Charred People?"

"You may call them that," Muhajji said. "The System may call them that. They call themselves the Inheritors."

"Inheritors of what?" Shari asked.

"There is no time to talk," Muhajji said, and looked nervously around. "There are wolves about. We must reach a place of sanctuary before it's too late."

"Sanctuary," Shari repeated and thought of Kristas. "We must find Kristas."

"I'm here," Kristas said, and they all turned to see him standing in a shaft of rainbow light filtered through one of the Abbey's stained-glass windows.

"Where have you been?" Cruse demanded.

"I had a headache," he said. "I needed to walk it off. . ."

Cruse grunted, obviously not believing him. "You're in for more walking them," he said, and pointed at Muhajji with his gun. "We're going off with our friend here."

"You trust me, then?" asked Muhajji.

"I want my skimmer repaired," was Cruse's non-committal reply.

"You still do not know what I want you to do for myself and the Inheritors," said Muhajji.

"We'll discuss it on the way."

"Where are we going, Muhajji?" asked Kristas, who came up to join the others. He didn't notice the sudden curious look that Cruse gave him.

"To the north of here," Muhajji replied. "It is too dangerous to travel overground, and there are tunnels we can use. The Inheritors say they are all that remains of this city's mass transport system. They call them the tubes. . ."

"Then lead on, Muhajji!" said Cruse with a cheeriness designed to mask his growing disquiet over Kristas.

Where had Kristas been, while he and Shari were meeting Muhajji? Kristas and Muhajji had not been introduced – so how did he know the stranger's name?

The Inheritors

The journey through the tunnels – the tubes as Muhajji called them – was a long and dank one. It was, however, also a relatively safe one, and, apart from a few rats which scrambled among the dirt and the rubble (the biggest rats any of them had ever seen), they were alone, their footsteps echoing down the passages like memories in an empty house.

Overground, Muhajji had told them, wolves were prowling, hungry for meat. Occasionally, System troopers would patrol the area, hunting down as many of the Inheritors as they could find. For some reason – Muhajji didn't know what – the Inheritors posed a threat to the System, but down here, in a network of tunnels which System records erroneously showed had been destroyed centuries ago, the Inheritors were safe.

"But who are the Charred People – I mean, the Inheritors?" Shari asked Muhajji, but the older man hushed her, as he led her out of the tunnel and into a huge chamber. A raised platform ran the length of the place and Muhajji helped first her and then Kristas on to the platform. Cruse needed no help and pulled himself up in one swift and fluid movement.

They looked around. The chamber was cavernous, with dirty tiled walls, its floor strewn with detritus, and its ceiling curved. Various archways led off to other chambers, or up to ancient-looking stairwells. It was primitive in the extreme, but dotted here and there were makeshift tents, although there was no sign of occupancy.

This chamber was only the latest in a series of similar chambers Muhajji had led them through. As Shari looked around she noticed a strange circular plaque on one of the walls. She crossed over to it, and wiped the dust off it to examine it more closely. The plaque was made of some metal, tarnished and rusted with age and damp. It was a large red circle, with a white centre and a blue horizontal bar bisecting it like some heraldic shield. On the bar were written the words:

KING'S CROSS
ST PANCRAS

Shari shrugged. The words seemed strangely familiar and she searched in her mind for them. Perhaps she had come across them during her ancient history classes? Failing to remember, she returned to her companions. Cruse was in the middle of a heated conversation with Muhajji, while Kristas, who had been showing signs of tiredness during the entire journey through the tubes, had sat down on a pile of sacking, near one of the tents.

"I think it's time you told us what you want from us, Muhajji," she heard Cruse say to the older man. "And something about the Inheritors, too."

Muhajji smiled and snapped his fingers. From out of each archway stepped several figures, dressed in rags like he was, until Cruse was surrounded. He instinctively reached down for his zip-gun, but didn't unholster it. He knew he was outnumbered, and, moreover, none of the strangers seemed hostile. Cruse chose to bide his time, but kept his hand on his gun.

There were about thirty newcomers in all, equally divided between the sexes, and their ages varied from a small boy, who Shari guessed to be about five, to an old man of about seventy, who leant on a stick, and was supported by a pretty young girl of about her own age.

They were all tall, much taller even than the six-feet-one Cruse, and their faces were, without exception, pale and ashen – the result, Shari guessed, of spending most of their lives living underground. The pupils of their eyes were abnormally large, presumably to let in as much light as possible so they could see in the darkened tubes. There was also a glazed look in those eyes; for a few moments Shari wondered whether they were all under the influence of some drug. Then she realized that the "glaze" in their eyes was due to a secondary, translucent eyelid, designed to shield their eyes from the harsh ultraviolet light from the sun on the surface.

Shari remembered all the horror stories about the Charred People – or the Inheritors as she now tried to call them. She had been prepared for hideous monsters, more horrible even than the mutants she, Cruse and Kristas had helped on the coasts. But apart from a certain detachment in their expressions, and the almost balletic way in which they silently moved, they looked very much the same as herself.

The old man on his stick stumbled forwards, helped by the young girl, and greeted Cruse. "You are welcome here, Cruse, you and your companions," he said. His voice was strong and clear, belying his infirm appearance.

Cruse wasted no time on social niceties. "You can repair my ship?" he demanded.

The old man nodded. "When men left the Earth, they also left behind them the machines they no longer needed. Over the years my people have collected them and stored them. The solar stacks will return power to your craft. They are still operational."

Cruse glanced at Shari. He had been right, after all.

The old man turned to a young man about Cruse's age, with a shock of rusty hair, and shoulders broader and more powerful than most of his fellows. "Barnaby here will see to it."

The man called Barnaby nodded in agreement, and left the chamber with several other young men.

"And what do you get out of the deal?" Cruse asked.

"Sanctuary," came the old man's reply. At mention of that word, Shari instinctively looked over at Kristas; he had fallen asleep in the corner on the bed of sacking.

"Sanctuary from what?" she asked, and approached the old man, who bowed his head in a gentlemanly welcome.

"From the System, what else?" he said.

"You seem to be safe enough from them down here," Cruse remarked. "I'd no idea that these tunnels existed."

"For the moment, yes, we are safe," the old man agreed. "And we have been safe from them for almost a thousand years..."

"Look, just who are you?" Shari interrupted. "I'd been told that only monsters inhabited the Wastes above ground. But you all look just like me!"

The old man chuckled. "That's because we *are* all just like you! Or at least we once were just like you."

"I'm sorry – I don't understand..."

"It's been a thousand years since the Great Colonial War when Wessex and the Kentish Moot poisoned the lands of the country once called England," the old man said wistfully. "A thousand years since the System came into being, and evacuated mankind's home planet, to forge a new empire in the solar system. But some of us loved our home, even though its rivers ran bitter with poisons and only a few dry shrubs grew in what used to be rich and fertile farmland. Some of us – not many – elected to stay behind."

"You're all a thousand years old?" Shari couldn't believe what she was hearing.

The old man chuckled. "Of course not, child," he said. "But all of us here are the descendants of those few people who chose not to desert their mother planet in its hour of need. The true inheritors of the Earth, you could say, rather than the Home Planet or whatever name the System gives it today.

"But if you've survived for so long, why do you need sanctuary from the System now?" Shari asked him, but it was Cruse who replied.

"Trueheart's taking an interest in the planet again, now that his popularity is falling," he said. "We've witnessed that, even though we're not quite sure why. He's already exterminating the mutants – getting rid of the evidence of his past mistakes, as well as feeding the System's bellies. Imagine what would happen if the people of the System discovered that a group of humans have been getting along very well, thank-you-very-much, without the help of the glorious System for a thousand years. It would be a marvellous propaganda coup against Trueheart; I doubt even that toadying flunky of his, the Child Roland, could contain that sort of damage. Now, more than ever before, the System President *is* the System. If Trueheart falls it might even signal the end of the System itself: it's in Trueheart's own interests to make sure that no one ever does find out."

"So you want us to help you escape the System?" Shari asked, and the old man nodded.

"It was Muhajji who told us of your existence," he said. "Muhajji has travelled over much of the country, and has heard tell of your helping the mutants flee the System."

"Lucky for you then that we happened to crashland in London," Cruse said thoughtfully, and stared curiously at Muhajji.

"It was indeed," Muhajji allowed, and pressed: "Will you help us?"

Shari looked over at Cruse, who nodded. "Of course we will," she said. "As soon as our skimmer is readied we can start transporting you and your people somewhere safe."

"If there is anywhere on the Earth that's safe now,"

said Cruse, ever the realist. "Trueheart's men are buzzing around this planet like a swarm of flies having a get-together over a dungheap!"

"There is one place where we could be safe," said the old man, and looked archly at Cruse. "One place where you, too, might be able to hide from the System. For ever..."

Cruse looked curiously at the old man, his interest aroused. However, he affected an air of nonchalance, hooking his fingers in the belt of his combat trousers. "And where might that be, then?" he drawled.

The young girl at the old man's side came up to him. "There is a place that we know as the Honeywell," she said.

"The Honeywell? What's that?" asked Shari. She looked over at Cruse who shook his head: he had never heard the name before either. He urged the girl to continue.

"It's a place of refuge and sanctuary," she explained. "Where the mutants, misfits and refugees can live in peace, hidden from the prying eyes of the System."

"The System's 'eyes', as you so quaintly call them, are everywhere," Cruse said practically. "No one can escape them for very long."

"The System's own people can," the girl said, and gave a smug smile, as she saw a look of intense interest flicker in Cruse's dark eyes. "The Honeywell was founded, and is still run by, a former System official, the highest-ranking person ever, so they say, to defect from the System. She knows how the System works — how Donovan Trueheart and the Child Roland work — and she knows how to confound their spying devices."

Cruse stroked his chin. "A defector?" he muttered, half to himself. He had heard of no top officials defecting in years, but then that was hardly surprising, given Roland's near-total control over all the System's information networks. But before the Child Roland had taken over the Ministry of Enlightenment, Cruse had heard rumours of many officials who had been dissatisfied in some way with the System. Perhaps he might have heard of this top-ranking official. "Who is she?" he demanded.

The girl shrugged. "No one knows her real name," she admitted. "But we call her Momma Mercy."

"Cute," was Cruse's sarcastic response.

"And she provides a refuge for the System's enemies?" Shari asked, and turned excitedly to Cruse. "Isn't that wonderful? We're not alone after all, Cruse; there are others working against the System too!"

Cruse continued to look at the young girl. "So what's in it for Momma Mercy?" was his by now predictable question. Shari flashed him an angry look, and tried to change the subject.

"Where is the Honeywell?" she asked the old man.

"Many klicks to the south-west of here," he said, and glanced towards one of the doorways, through which Barnaby was returning. "Barnaby knows the exact location."

Barnaby smiled at Cruse and Shari. "The solar stacks will soon be ready to be taken to your craft," he said.

"Thank you, Barnaby," said Shari, and, when she saw that Cruse wasn't prepared to offer his own thanks, added pointedly: "From both of us." She looked at the old man and the girl. "We know Barnaby's name, and Muhajji's," she remarked. "But what are you called?"

The old man smiled. "They call me Mayor Casterbridge, or Casterbridge for short," he said, and looked over at the young girl. "And this is my niece – Alice Liddell."

"Strange names," Cruse remarked.

"They are names which have been passed down through the generations," Casterbridge said.

"As has my own full name," said Barnaby. "Barnaby Rudge." He turned to Cruse. "I have a map in my quarters which shows the location of the Honeywell," he said, and motioned for Cruse, Casterbridge and Muhajji to follow him out of the chamber, Cruse did so, but not before asking Shari to remain behind.

When they had gone, Alice turned to Shari and

smiled. "Is your friend always so gloomy?" she asked.

Shari laughed, suddenly realizing that it had been a long time since she had had a gossip with a girl her own age; most of the time she was too busy trying to keep the peace between Cruse and Kristas. "Once I caught him smiling!" she joked.

"He's been unlucky in love," Alice said abruptly. "He's been hurt so much that he can't bring himself to trust anyone ever again."

Shari frowned, suddenly serious. "You're right," she said, "but how could you possibly know that?"

"I know," was all Alice could say, unconsciously echoing Kristas's earlier words. Alice look over at Kristas: he was still sleeping on the sacking. "Is your friend all right?" she asked anxiously.

"He's not been feeling too well," Shari admitted. "He's been having a lot of headaches lately: I'm worried about him..."

A glance passed between the two girls: they both knew of the plagues and diseases which infested the land above their heads. "I'm sure he'll be all right," Alice reassured Shari with a confidence she did not feel.

The two girls walked over to Kristas, and looked down at him. His face, normally tanned and healthy, was now pale, as white as the chalk cliffs he and Shari had scaled the previous night. There was a thin sheen of sweat on his forehead, but the front of his tunic was dark and sodden with perspiration.

Shari reached out a hand and felt Kristas's brow: it was as cold as ice. She and Alice exchanged a worried look. Kristas was muttering something, and she leant down in an attempt to hear him. Suddenly Kristas's eyes snapped open, and he sat up and grabbed Shari's arm.

"Kristas! What is it?" Shari gasped; she had never seen the wild look in Kristas's eyes before. She felt the touch of his hand against her skin: he was freezing.

"Alone ... so alone..." he muttered. "So frightened..."

"Hush, Kristas, you're not alone, you're with us now, with the Inheritors," Shari said softly and hugged him tightly.

"No, not me..." Kristas shook his head. "A thousand voices, crying in the darkness..."

"He's rambling," said Alice. "I've seen it happen before ... when people have contracted the fever...'

"It's not the fever," Shari protested.

Kristas has not caught a fever. He is not going to die! she said over and over to herself, even though she no longer believed it. She looked her old friend straight in the eyes.

"If it's not you, Kristas, who is it? Who's alone? Who's frightened?"

Suddenly Kristas stopped shivering, and a warm

glow returned to his cheeks. There was terror in his eyes, as he looked, not at Shari, but at Alice.

"Who's alone?" Alice repeated the question. "Who's frightened?"

"Don't you, of all people, know?" he asked. "It's the Other..."

The Magnificent Donovan Trueheart threw back his head and finished yet another glass of wine. Two empty bottles already stood on his mahogany desk, witness to the latest of the drinking bouts in which the System President had recently been indulging, to the detriment of his fast-thickening waistline. At his feet, Gabriel eyed his master apprehensively: the Trueheart had been so drunk last night that he had passed out at his desk and had forgotten to feed him.

The door to the Trueheart's chamber opened and the Child Roland entered. He cast his eyes over the office, and assessed the situation in an instant. He smiled wryly to himself, and marched briskly over to Trueheart. Gabriel growled a welcome; at least the Child ensured that he never went hungry.

Gabriel loved the Child Roland.

"Your Magnificence is tired," the Child Roland remarked, and tried not to turn away from the vinegary fumes on the Trueheart's breath as Donovan looked at him. "Perhaps it would be best if you were to retire to bed?"

The Trueheart tried to stand up, discovered that it

was not such a good idea after all, and remained sitting (and poured himself another glass of wine).

"Nonsense, Roland," he said, making an enormous and largely successful effort not to slur his words. "How runs the System today?"

Roland affected a reluctant air, as if he didn't want to upset his leader further, but nevertheless pulled his smart-box out of his tunic, and consulted it.

"Not at optimum performance level, I'm afraid, Your Magnificence," he said, his voice conveying just the right amount of concern.

"More protests against myself, I suppose," the Trueheart said wearily, and regarded his reflection in the dark-red of his wine. "More despicable ingrates whingeing that they haven't enough to eat or drink." He threw back his wine, before looking up at the Child Roland. "Why do they hate me so, Roland? Why are they so dissatisfied with their lot?"

"I'm sure I don't know, Your Magnificence," Roland said, and examined a pink stain on his otherwise spotless white tunic: he must have dropped a piece of food during dinner this evening. He licked his lips in memory of that particularly fine lobster in a rich creamy sauce of genetically-bred prawns and shallots.

"Do I not give them all they need?" the Trueheart asked, in the declamatory style he used for his rare public addresses. "Do I not grieve when they grieve? Do I not go hungry when they go hungry?" He reached for a chicken-leg on the plate on his desk, and chomped greedily on it.

"Indeed you do, your Magnificence," was Roland's loyal reply.

"Then *why*, Roland?" asked the Trueheart, who was now close to drunken tears. "Why do they turn against me?"

Because they do not have enough to eat. Because more and more people are setting an example by doing the unthinkable and escaping from the System. People like Shari Sharifi, and her friends Cruse and Kristas Chernenko.

Especially Kristas Chernenko. Don't think that I don't know why we – you – need Kristas Chernenko.

That was what the wily Child Roland thought. What he said, however, was: "I'm sure I don't understand such ingratitude, Your Magnificence. But rest assured that their numbers are very small indeed, and that most of the people love you with all their heart."

Donovan Trueheart eyed the Child Roland suspiciously, but chose to accept the lie.

"If you wish to regain the affection and renewed loyalty of this – this absurdly small number of malcontents," said Roland, "then perhaps I could arrange an incident. . ."

"An incident?" The Trueheart was interested now: whenever things were going badly he knew that he could always rely on the Child Roland to provide an "incident".

"There could be an accident," the Child Roland suggested. "An interplanetary freighter shot down in mid-flight, perhaps. Or better still, an explosion in one of the nuclear reactors on TerraNova – a long way from Your Magnificence's vineyards, of course. We wouldn't want to deprive Your Magnificence of one of his very few pleasures in this life."

"Of course not," agreed the Trueheart. "Radioactive fallout can do such strange things to the fruits of the vine."

"We would say that it was the work of an anti-System terrorist group, and Your Magnificence could then go in and comfort the survivors," Roland continued. "It would make for marvellous coverage on all the main news networks."

"Would many people be killed?" the Trueheart asked, and drummed his fingers on the desk, considering Roland's suggestion.

The Child Roland shrugged. "A few hundred at the most," he replied. "Perhaps even fewer if children were involved: after all, one slaughtered child receives far greater media coverage than ten assassinated adults. It is a small price to pay for Your Magnificence's peace of mind."

Donovan Trueheart stood up, swayed drunkenly, and gave the Child Roland an avuncular pat on the back. "As usual, Roland, you think too small," he said. "That is why I am the System President, and you are merely my Minister for Enlightenment."

"I would be honoured to be even the smallest minion in the furthest outpost of Your Magnificence's great empire," the Child Roland lied. "What do you suggest?"

"Pasiphae – one of the moons of Jupiter," said the Trueheart, and there was an evil glint in his green eyes. "Its destruction would sicken and horrify the entire System – and win the people over to my side, when I order the ruthless tracking down of the terrorists responsible for this vile deed!"

The Child Roland's face went pale. "An entire planetoid, Your Magnificence?" he asked. He checked his smart-box for the current population of Pasiphae. "Two million innocent people?"

The Trueheart gazed angrily at his aide-de-camp. "I am Donovan Trueheart, am I not?" he asked. "And I can do what I like?"

The Child Roland bowed his head in acquiescence. "Of course, Your Magnificence. I shall contact Commander Schreck immediately. I'm sure he will enjoy conducting the operation."

Donovan Trueheart grinned. "There's a wonderful symmetry about it, Roland, you see," he said. "Pasiphae is the home world of Shari Sharifi and Kristas Chernenko. They may not have been among the first to question the values of the System, but they have become a symbol for our disaffected and misguided youth; it's only right that their home should be the first to fall to our wrath. And besides, production levels have fallen on that planet. It's a drain on the System's resources..."

The Child Roland shivered: even he was incapable of such callousness. Yet while he despaired of the Trueheart's plans, the Child Roland was already considering ways in which he could use them to his own personal advantage. (And for the good of the System, of course.)

Donovan Trueheart returned to his desk: he needed another drink. He slugged one back, and stared into space for a few moments. "The power of life and death, to make the dead live again, that is the power of a god, is it not, Roland?" he asked.

"Indeed it is, Your Magnificence," Roland replied. "Since you mentioned the concept of godhead to me the other day I've been doing much reading around the subject – a fascinating notion, and one totally suited to Your Magnificence's great talents..."

"And like all gods, I demand a sacrifice," the Trueheart rambled on.

"Pasiphae?"

The Trueheart shook his head. "That is merely a means to make the people take me to their hearts again," he said. "Those three meddlesome brats, Roland..."

The Child nodded. "Everything is going according to plan," he said.

98

"Excellent," said the Trueheart. "To raise the dead is no difficult matter – a god just needs fresh blood. And one of those brats will provide that blood!"

Roland frowned. "Your Magnificence is, of course, speaking metaphorically?" he asked.

"Am I, Roland?" smiled the Trueheart. His head slumped, and the revered System President fell face-forwards on to his desk, totally drunk.

Roland sighed and made sure the Trueheart was comfortable, then took away his dinner plate. He placed it on the floor by the desk, where Gabriel pounced on it greedily.

For a second, the Child Roland looked sadly at the spectacle of the Trueheart, dishevelled and drunken at his desk. It seemed a pity that such a great man should have been brought so low. Then the Child Roland checked himself; he was letting his emotions run away with him, and that would never do.

Besides, when you have to organize the deaths of two million people, and ensure that three other individuals remain very much alive, you simply cannot let your emotions get in the way.

The Inheritance

Cruse checked the on-board flight computer and nodded to himself, satisfied with the skimmer's performance. The power stacks which Barnaby Rudge had provided seemed to be compatible with the skimmer's engines, even though they had to be at least eight hundred years old. When Cruse had asked Barnaby why the Inheritors had never thought to use the stacks to construct their own ships, he had told him that his people had eschewed technology many generations ago.

They had a point, Cruse allowed. After the devastation that technology had visited on the Earth, he could understand them not wanting to use anything more complicated than a bow and arrow ever again.

But without a zip-gun at his side, Cruse only felt half a man.

Shari was by his side, acting as co-pilot, although Cruse's skills were so good that she was scarcely needed. Behind them in the cabin were about fifteen of the Inheritors – the skimmer was too small to accommodate any more, and Cruse and Shari had arranged to return later for the others.

Amongst them were Muhajji, Casterbridge and Barnaby, their pale ashen faces and rags a stark contrast to the sleek, if slightly run-down, appearance of the cabin. Kristas had remained behind with Alice, and was due to come over with the next group. He was still running a fever, and Alice was caring for him.

"A cold, that's all it is," Shari had said over and over again, when they had left him. "A minor infection, nothing more..." And, while Cruse had pretended to agree with her, he suspected in his heart of hearts that neither of them would ever see Kristas alive again.

Barnaby came up to the flight deck, and peered over Cruse's shoulder at the navigational controls, and the scanner, which would alert them to the presence of any other craft in the vicinity – System hunter-ships.

"Are we nearly there?" he asked, with all the anticipation of a child being taken on holiday by his parents.

"Ten minutes," Cruse said, without turning round. "That is, if the co-ordinates on that map you gave me are right." He glanced at the sheet of circular metal plate which Barnaby had handed to him at the beginning of their journey.

"The map is one of our most sacred artefacts, which has been handed down through the generations," Barnaby said, shocked that Cruse should even think to call its accuracy into question. "Of course it's right..."

"It's just a pity that it doesn't tell us the exact location of the Honeywell," Shari said.

"How could it?" Barnaby said. "The map comes from before the War. The Honeywell has been around for seventy years at most. But we do know that the Honeywell is located near the Stones – and they are pin-pointed on the map."

"Where exactly are we, Cruse?" Shari asked. The part of the country over which they were flying was unfamiliar to her.

"What does it matter?" Cruse said. "One blighted and barren waste is very much like any other blighted and barren waste!"

"*Cruse,*" Shari reproved, and the mercenary grinned.

"We're over what used to be Wessex," he informed her, and adjusted a control, to prepare the skimmer for descent. "Ironic, isn't it, that the Honeywell should be located in the very heartland of one of the republics that started the Great Colonial Wars.''

"A war which was indirectly responsible for bringing about the foundation of the System," said Muhajji, who had come up to join them. "And now the Honeywell is working against that very same System... There's a sort of justice there..."

Cruse laughed. "You see, Shari, there is a God after all!"

Shari picked up the map from the flight deck and examined it, reading the names of long-forgotten towns and cities, their millions of inhabitants wiped off the face of the Earth by all the System's petty wars. Bristol, Bath, Glastonbury, Salisbury. She wondered what life must have been like in those towns, before the wars, before the System.

"Where did this map come from, Barnaby?" she asked, after she had replaced it on the flight deck.

"They say our ancestors found it in the wastes, after the War," he said. "In the rubble, above King's-Cross-Saint-Pancras. It was there that we also found our Inheritance...'

Cruse growled. This was a sore point with him. "A bloody wooden box!" he said. "Do you realize just how much space tht blasted thing is taking up – we could have got two more people in here if not for that!"

Shari hushed him, and looked towards the back of the cabin. An ornate wooden box, about two metres long and one metre high and wide, and inlaid with fine gold filigree, had been placed there. Casterbridge was standing by it, leaning on his stick, presiding over the box, just as the guard of honour must have done over King William's tomb all those long centuries ago in Westminster Abbey.

"It's the Inheritors' most sacred relic," Muhajji explained. "It goes everywhere with them."

"You're not an Inheritor, Muhajji," Cruse reminded him. "Why should it mean anything to you?"

"My identity is a secret – even to myself. But the Inheritors saved my life once and now I respect their traditions and beliefs."

"It weighs a bloody ton!" Cruse moaned – he had had to help Barnaby carry it on board the skimmer. He glanced back at the young man. "What's in it, Barnaby?"

"Our Inheritance," Barnaby repeated. "A source of limitless power, so they say, from the days before the War..."

"'Limitless power', eh?" Cruse said. He liked the sound of that. He turned round, after instructing Shari to watch over the flight controls for a moment. "Now that sounds interesting. I could do with something to knock out the System. What sort of limitless power?"

"We don't know," Barnaby said simply.

"You mean you haven't opened the box to find out?" Cruse asked in disbelief.

"The box is locked, and we have no key," Barnaby explained patiently.

"So break it open!" Cruse snapped, losing his temper. He felt Muhajji lay a calming hand on his shoulder.

"To break the box would go against all that the Inheritors believe in, Cruse," he told him. "Their legends say that the key to the box will be found, but only when the time is ready. Until then it must remain closed."

Cruse groaned with exasperation, and returned to the controls. "You people are crazy!" he declaimed. "System knows why I'm even helping you!"

Shari smiled and exchanged a glance with Muhajji: they both knew why he was helping the Inheritors. It wasn't just that he hated the System, and Trueheart especially, and would do anything to harm them. The idea of the Honeywell – an entire community fighting the System from a position of safety – had entrapped him, just as surely as a fly is caught in a spider's web.

"We are grateful for your help, Cruse," Barnaby said. "Please try and understand our traditions. . ."

"Weirdos," Cruse muttered, not quite under his breath.

"Cruse! Look!" Barnaby suddenly exclaimed in panic: he pointed to the gridded screen of the flight-path indicator.

"What's wrong?" Cruse asked, and peered at the screen. "There's nothing there!"

"Yes, there is!" Barnaby insisted. "Can't you see those two blips on the screen? Two other craft, approaching fast!"

Shari and Muhajji took it in turns to look at the screen. It was blank. "There's nothing there," Shari said. "You're imagining it."

"No, they're definitely there," Barnaby insisted and continued to stare at the screen.

And then, almost as if Barnaby had willed them into existence, the two blips appeared on the screen. Cruse immediately flicked over to visual, and the stubby black shapes of two System hunter-ships came into view.

"He's right!" he cried. "Shari, take evasive action now!"

Shari's hands were already flitting over the navigational control. Adrenalin coursed through her body, preparing her for the airborne chase and battle she knew was sure to follow in only a few seconds' time.

And then she stopped.

"Shari, you little idiot!" cursed Cruse. "What are you doing? Let's get the hell out of here!"

"There's no need, Cruse," she said calmly, and pointed to the screen. The two hunter-ships were veering off away from them. Within seconds they were no more than two black pinpricks silhouetted against the 'O'-shape of the full moon.

Cruse leant back in his pilot's seat, and stared at the

screen. "I don't believe it!" he gasped. "They must have seen us! Why didn't they attack? It was almost as if they were trying to avoid us..."

"Are we safe now?" Muhajji asked anxiously.

Cruse nodded, and engaged the skimmer's main thrust to descend. "I don't like this – it's as if someone wanted to keep us alive..."

"I'm not complaining," said Barnaby, and was surprised when Cruse turned around and stared at him evilly.

"And you saw those hunters coming at us when they were still out of range," he said slowly. "Before any of us saw them."

"That's right," Barnaby said. "I don't understand why you and Shari and Muhajji didn't see them."

"Neither do I," Cruse said. "But I intend to find out!"

Alice looked down fondly on Kristas's sleeping face, and removed a strand of hair from his closed eyes. It was nearly morning now, and Alice had been watching over him for most of the night, raising a glass of water to his parched lips those times when he briefly woke and needed it, mopping up the sweat from his brow with a swathe of by-now sodden cloth.

Kristas had been shivering uncontrollably for most of the night, and yet he had a red-hot temperature. All his body functions seemed to be raging out of control:

only a few hours ago when she had held his hand to feel his pulse, (much faster than it should have been), he had been ice-cold.

Even though he had been asleep his lips had been moving soundlessly all night long; occasionally Alice had leant down to try and hear whatever words he might have been trying to say, but all she could hear were a series of painful and long drawn-out groans, and Kristas's heavy and frantic breathing. He was like a drowning man, trying desperately to suck in one more mouthful of air before he went down for the third and final time.

Finally he woke up, to see Alice smiling down at him.

"How are you feeling?" she asked, struggling to check the sadness in her voice.

Kristas gave her a weak smile. "Better – I think," he breathed. "Have I been asleep for long?"

"Hours," she said. "You missed the others' departure. Cruse and Shari have gone off to the Honeywell."

"They won't come back here," Kristas said. There was no emotion in the comment. It was a simple statement of fact.

"Of course they will," Alice reassured him. "They promised they would take us and all the others to the Honeywell – to sanctuary."

Kristas shook his head. "Where are the others?" he asked, and sat up. He and Alice were in a small anteroom, off the main section of tunnels. A tarnished metal plate on one of the tiled walls read: STAFF REST ROOM.

"They're in Viktoriline," she said referring to the name they had given to one of the tunnels. "They thought you would be better off here."

"They must leave the tubes now!" Kristas said, and attempted to stand up. His legs were too weak and he fell back down on his bedding of sackcloths.

"Don't be silly," Alice said. "You know we can't leave the tubes. Down here we're safe from the wolves and the poison mists and the System."

"*Nonono*," Kristas said. "We're not safe here any more." He moaned and raised a trembling hand to his head. "My head hurts, Alice. It feels like it might explode any second."

"Try and get some sleep, Kristas."

"No, that's even worse," he said, starting to sob. "You can't understand the dreams I have when I'm asleep. Strange things reaching out for me, trying to tear my skin from me, layer by layer like you would an onion. Ripping out my insides, trying to eat into my brain. Shadows calling out my name. Millions of people crying out in agony, as the bomb drops on them and turns them all to ash. And there there's the Other..."

Alice frowned. "You mentioned the Other before, Kristas. What is the Other?"

Kristas shrugged. "The Other ... is the Other. He's calling out to me. Can't you hear him?"

Alice paused, remembering the nightmares she had sometimes had as a child. There had been times when she thought someone had been calling her name, trying to rouse her from her sleep. But when she had awoken, her room had always been empty. Casterbridge had just smiled indulgently and told her that she was simply highly-strung. She'd believed that, and, as she grew up, as she became a "responsible" member of her small community, so she trained herself to ignore those whispers in her dreams. She shook her head.

"No, Kristas, I can't hear them," she said.

"He's hurting," Kristas said. "He needs me – without me he is not whole. And I can't do anything for him..."

Alice cradled Kristas's head in her arms, crooning to him like a mother would to a new-born child. Soon Kristas stopped crying, even though his head was aching like it had never ached before. His eyes grew misty as white lights seemed to dance and flash before him, and the only sound he could hear was the insistent *thud-thud-thud* of his own heartbeat. The pain was so great that he couldn't even consider his own fate, couldn't even wonder whether he was going to live or to die; all Kristas's energies were now concentrated on trying to shut out as much of this terrible thundering as possible.

"You'll get better soon, you'll see," Alice said. "Once we get to the Honeywell..."

They sat there in silence for several minutes, each of them wrapped up in their own thoughts. Alice prayed that Kristas hadn't caught the plague, but he seemed to show all the symptoms. It was only by remaining in these underground tunnels for generations upon generations that her own people had managed to remain disease-free; if Kristas had the plague, then what was there to say that he hadn't already unknowingly infected her and her friends?

They had to get to the Honeywell as soon as possible. Momma Mercy would know what to do, Momma Mercy would make them all well again. She felt Kristas shiver once more in her arms, and debated whether she should leave him to fetch another blanket.

"No, don't bother yourself, Alice," Kristas said. "I don't need another blanket. I'm not cold – I'll be fine."

"What?"

"You asked me if I needed another blanket," he said. "You needn't bother."

Alice stared at Kristas, and a devastating idea suggested itself to her.

"Kristas, I didn't say a thing," she said through trembling lips. "I didn't say a word."

"Don't be silly," Kristas said. "Of course you did. I heard you as clear as a bell."

Alice shook her head. "I didn't *say* those words," she repeated. "I *thought* them!"

Shari had taken a cape from the skimmer and now she pulled it closely around her, shivering in the cold and surveying the plain before her. It seemed to stretch on for miles, wasted and wild, the ash which covered it gleaming spookily in the full moonlight.

And in the centre of it was the ring of stones, about twenty or thirty of them, black and monolithic, lording over the landscape like silent frozen warriors. Despite everything, there was a serenity about this place, similar to the sense of peace and sanctuary they had all experienced back there in the ruins of Westminster Abbey.

Cruse came out of the skimmer, and joined Shari and the others who had disembarked. He looked around, clearly unimpressed by what he saw.

"This is the place on the map you gave me," he told Barnaby. "So where's the Honeywell?"

"Near here," Barnaby said. "We will find it in time..."

"On a plain hundreds of klicks wide?" he said. "Tell me another one..."

"We will find it," said Casterbridge. "Our thoughts will seek it out."

"Your thoughts?" Cruse was intrigued. "You mean, you're all telepathic?" he asked, but Casterbridge smiled and shook his head.

"Rather say we have a keener instinct than people such as yourselves who were born within the System," he explained. "We developed it over the long years to survive out there in the Wastes."

"Having a well-developed sense of danger is one thing," Cruse said, unimpressed. "Using that sense to seek out a place you've never been to before is another."

"Have you never seen a lupe, returning to its home, after being abandoned by its masters in a distant foreign town?" Barnaby asked. "They say that salmon would return every year to their breeding grounds – that was when there were salmon in the rivers, of course."

"I'd much prefer a map," Cruse said. "We'd best return to the skimmer – we'll find nothing here until it's light."

"At least there are no poison mists here," Casterbridge remarked, and sniffed the air. "In fact, the atmosphere smells remarkably unpolluted."

"Cruse, come over here," Shari called out, and he turned to look at her. She was kneeling down by one of the large stones which formed the outer perimeter of the circle; a shadowy bulk lay at her feet.

"What is it?" she asked him when he came over. The thing at her feet was dead, which was just as well, as alive she could imagine it killing her before she had even registered its presence. It was about the size and shape of a horse, but it had a long shaggy mane, sabre-sharp molars which looked as if they could tear open a carcass as easily as Shari or Cruse could a paper bag, and limbs which, in life, must have rippled with solid and powerful muscle.

"An ugly old brute," was Cruse's initial reaction. He called Muhajji and Barnaby over, neither of whom had seen a similar creature before.

"Could it have evolved over the centuries into that?" Barnaby asked. "Adapting itself to the changing environmental circumstances? The wolves did in London; so did we to survive."

"Maybe," said Cruse, although it was evident that he didn't give much weight to Barnaby's theory. "I'm no biologist but I don't think that an animal could develop so much in only nine hundred or so years. There's no way that this could be the product of evolution – not *natural* evolution, anyway…"

"You mean you think it's a mutated species?" asked Shari. "Like the human mutants we've met here on Earth – the result of the System's genetic experiments?"

"That's more likely, apart from one thing," said Cruse. "Trueheart's got a soft spot for all animals – genetic experimentation on our fluffy friends is strictly forbidden."

"Well, it must have come from somewhere," Shari reasoned.

"What I'm more worried about is where its play-mates are," Cruse said and stood up. He turned to the others. "We go back to the skimmer," he announced authoritatively. "We start looking for this Honeywell in the morning – although the chances of finding it in this wilderness are – look out!"

Cruse ripped his zip-gun out of its holster, and trained it on the shadowy figures who had suddenly just stepped out of their hiding places behind the large stones. Shari did the same, but it was all in vain. They were surrounded on all sides, and twenty laser-rifles were aimed at them. Acknowledging defeat, Cruse and Shari dropped their guns to their sides.

There was a frightened murmur amongst the Inheritors as their ambushers stepped into the moonlight to reveal their faces: few of the Inheritors had seen such freaks before in even their wildest nightmares.

There was a man, totally bald, part of whose scalp had been removed and his brain exposed, pumping and throbbing under a protective plastic dome; another woman had a face covered with running sores; the face of another had been blown half away, and a mangled mess of wires and plates covered the left side of his face; others looked more animal than human.

"Mutes," Cruse said under his breath, and they regarded him with narrow, suspicious eyes (those who had eyes, that is: the nostrils of the eyeless others twitched in his direction, like hyenas scenting the smell of death).

"Don't be afraid," said Shari. "We won't hurt you."

"But will they harm us?" Cruse asked as the mutants drew even nearer. They both knew that the minds of many of the System's mutants had been so much destroyed by their experiences at the hands of the System's geneticists that they had become paranoid and dangerous.

"We're Cruse and Shari Sharifi," Shari said. "Surely you've heard of us? We help mutants –" she corrected herself – '*people* like yourselves to escape from the System..."

The mutants muttered amongst themselves at the mention of the hated word.

Muhajji looked curiously at the mutants, and a faint glimmer of recognition appeared briefly in his eyes. He tried to remember; but no matter how hard he tried, his life before the Inheritors found him on the banks of the Thames was a total blank, as if he had never existed before that time.

"They're speaking the truth," he said finally. "Neither they nor the Inheritors wish you any harm. All they want is sanctuary..."

"Sanctuary..." The mutants repeated the word in their dry and raspy voices. "Sanctuary... Sanctuary..."

The tallest of the mutants – the one whose brain was partly exposed, and who seemed to be the leader – stepped forward. Shari took an involuntary step back and her hand tightened automatically on her zip-gun.

"Cruse and Shari," the creature repeated, and looked carefully at both of them. Shari was reminded of the wolf in the Wastes, as it leapt on to her; the same sort of fiery determination and hunger was in the tall mutant's eyes too. "You are seeking sanctuary?"

"Yes," said Shari.

"They call me Ganymede,' said the wizened, ugly leader of the mutants, all of whom still kept their laser-rifles trained on them.

Where had they found such weapons? Cruse wondered. The mutants they had encountered before were shy and wary creatures, more willing to cower away from System patrols than attack them and seize their weapons.

"You are right," Ganymede continued. "We have heard of refugees from the System who have helped our brother- and sister-mutants escape the revenge of Donovan Trueheart..."

"That's us," Shari said.

"We have also heard that there are three of you," Ganymede continued, not bothering to hide his suspicions.

"Yes – there's Kristas," Shari said. "You must help us – he's sick..."

"Then if he is sick, he will die," Ganymede said, no trace of emotion in his voice; he might have been commenting on the weather for all the feeling he showed. "All who catch the plague perish eventually. It is sad, but that is the way of things here on the Earth."

"*No*," said Shari firmly; and Cruse reached out and held her hand, in a gesture of friendship and support.

Ganymede seemed unmoved by Shari's outburst; instead he considered the Inheritors – Barnaby, Casterbridge and the rest, as well as Muhajji, all of whom, up to now, had remained silent. "These are friends of yours?" he asked Cruse.

"Well –" Cruse began, unsurely, but Shari interrupted him.

"Yes," she said firmly. "*Good* friends of ours."

"We have your word, Shari Sharifi?"

"Of course."

Ganymede nodded, satisfied. "Then you shall come with us – to sanctuary." He made a sign to his fellow Mutes, and they all lowered their rifles. Ganymede started to move away, and signalled Shari, Cruse and the others to follow him.

"But what about the Inheritance?" Barnaby said. The wooden box was still in the skimmer, and had not been taken out when Cruse had landed the craft.

Ganymede looked interested – *just a little too interested*, thought Cruse. "The Inheritance?" he asked. "This is something precious to you?"

"Yes –"

"No," Cruse said quickly, and walked up close to

Ganymede, affecting an air of camaraderie. "Just a little piece of nonsense – superstitious twaddle – you know the sort of thing. . ."

Ganymede smiled a supercilious and indulgent smile. "It will be safe here," he promised them. "The Plain of Stones is dead – apart from those creatures. . ." He looked down at the carcass of the animal Shari had discovered.

"Where did that come from?" asked Barnaby. "I've never seen creatures like that before."

Ganymede frowned, and Barnaby winced as the mutant's exposed cerebrum throbbed as it thought hard, trying to remember. "They have always been here, scavenging for food around the plains," he said.

"Things grow here?" asked Shari, instantly remembering what Kristas had told her: You can't defeat Mother Nature, Shari: she always wins through in the end. . .

"Of course," said Ganymede. "Why shouldn't they? Momma loves gardening, and she is very good to us. . ."

"Momma?"

Ganymede nodded, unsure of what all the fuss was about. "Momma gives us all we need and we love our Momma," he said.

"Momma Mercy?" Barnaby found it difficult to contain his emotions. "You're from the Honeywell? It really exists?"

Ganymede seemed bemused by the look of

disbelieving joy on Barnaby's face. "Where else would we come from?" he asked. "There is nothing else on this Plain, except for the stones." He started to move off and beckoned Shari and Cruse and the others to follow them. "Come with us. Momma is waiting for us all at the Honeywell."

Shari glanced at Cruse who nodded, and they and the Inheritors started to follow the mutants.

"We'll come with you," said Cruse. "But after that we're returning for Kristas and the others."

"As you wish," said Ganymede pleasantly. "But your friend will already be dead."

"Momma Mercy can help him," Shari insisted.

"Perhaps..." said Ganymede. "We shall ask her."

And with that the entire company left the circle of stones – the palaeolithic monument that men had once called Stonehenge – and started their long trek across the great Plain. So concerned were they with their own thoughts – the Inheritors' relief at having found sanctuary, Shari's worries about Kristas, and Cruse's suspicion that everything wasn't quite as it should be – that none of them remarked that the ground beneath their feet was trembling, like an ancient underground beast about to arise from its ages-long sleep and wreak its revenge on the world.

Momma Mercy

$\mathbb{S}$hari woke up and wiped the sleep from her eyes. For a moment she thought she was back on her home world of Pasiphae, waking up in her own bed, and she half expected Kili, her robotic servant, to walk through the door, fussing and clucking like an old woman, and bringing her an invigorating morning beverage.

Then she remembered that Kili was long dead, and that even if she had wanted to return to Pasiphae she wouldn't have been able to: the System would have captured her the minute she achieved planet-fall.

She sat up, and rubbed her arm: there was a small rash just above her right elbow, and she assumed that she had scratched herself in the night. She looked around. She was sitting on a soft featherdown bed, a bowl of roses on her bedside table. A platter of bread and cheeses and fresh meats had been laid out for her, and over the chair had been hung freshly-laundered clothes, which she pulled on, and then she nibbled at the food: she had tasted nothing better in a long, long time.

Dawn had been breaking when they had reached the Honeywell; and, if Ganymede and mutants hadn't been guiding them, Shari was sure she would have missed it. Two huge double doors had been carved into the cleft of a hill, so successfully camouflaged in the reddish-brown colours of the surrounding countryside that Shari wasn't surprised that System hunter-ships had been unable to spot it on their periodic swoops of the area.

The doors had led them down a long tunnel, the gleamingly white walls of which were studded with thousands upon thousands of coloured lights, which blinked and twinkled, creating something of a minor soporific effect on them, as they followed Ganymede into the depths of the Earth.

After about twenty minutes' walk, the tunnel opened out on to a gantry, overlooking the first in a series of vast caverns. From here they could look down and survey the Honeywell. It was enormous, much grander than Shari and Cruse had ever expected, and Ganymede told them that the complex stretched for many klicks underground.

The "bottom" of the Honeywell was lost to the

eye, so far below them was it. From the ground, huge metal towers rose, climbing up the walls of the enormous cavern in which the Honeywell had been built. Each tower had many storeys and they were all connected to each other by gantries, along which shambled mutants similar to Ganymede and the others.

Shari could see other people too, on the gantries, or behind the windows of the towers: brisk-looking people, all about her and Cruse's age, going about their business. She caught the eye of one of them in the nearest tower, and he grinned and waved at her, before returning to his work. He was exceptionally good-looking, Shari decided, as indeed were all his colleagues; but then, she supposed that next to the mutants anyone would have appeared handsome.

Awe-inspiring though all this was, there was something else which impressed all of them even more. There was a sweet, magic tang in the air, which they breathed in deeply till it made them feel giddy: fresh air, so they imagined, unpolluted by the System's engines and technology. It smelt of roses.

Yet even this paled into insignificance next to something else, something Shari and Cruse, Muhajji and the Inheritors had never thought they would ever see again in their lives.

Greenness. Greenness everywhere, from the hanging gardens which seemed to grow on every gantry, to the arboretums of sturdy fine-leafed trees on every other level. It was an explosion of colour, of naturalness, and of a time before the System repainted every thing in varying shades of functional grey. And there was a strange sound in the air too, and when they looked for its source they saw swallows flitting from tree to tree, from flower to flower.

"It's beautiful," was all Shari could think of to say.

Even Cruse was impressed, almost to tears, but he looked at Ganymede and asked. "How can they grow underground?"

"Artificial sunlight," Ganymede said, and pointed up towards the roof of the Honeywell. The light emanating from there did look like sunlight, or rather sunlight as Cruse had imagined it to be, before the System blasted the ozone layer. "Also special bio-nutrients in the soil in which they are planted. Momma has very green fingers..."

"And Momma Mercy has given you all this?" Casterbridge marvelled.

Ganymede nodded. "Momma Mercy gives us all we need and we love our Momma," he said, repeating the words he had said earlier that night.

"I'd like to meet Momma Mercy," Cruse said, and Ganymede said that he would see her soon. Momma already knew of their arrival, he told him, and, after they had rested, they would be granted an audience with her.

So it was that Shari found herself in the small

124

bedroom which had been provided for her, in one of the lower levels of the Honeywell, in a complex which had been built around a beautiful arboretum of tall, strong trees, and through which ran a small stream of clear crystalline water, in which she even spotted a few fish.

There was a knock on her door, and she opened it to find Cruse standing there. He had washed and shaved, but she noticed that he was still wearing his combat fatigues, even though she guessed that fresh and clean clothes would have been put out for him as well.

"Good morning," she said dreamily. "Did you sleep well?"

Cruse grimaced. "Too well," he replied. "The deepest sleep I've had in a long time. I don't like that – it leaves you open, vulnerable."

"Some people are never satisfied," Shari pouted. "Sometimes I think you'll never be happy unless you're sleeping on a bed of nails!"

Cruse allowed himself a little self-deprecating grin. "It's good for the soul," he said. "I've been doing some snooping while you've been wasting your time in bed," he said.

"And?"

"The happiest, most beautiful place I've ever seen," he said, almost begrudgingly. "There are thousands of mutants here, all singing the praises of

Momma Mercy who's rescued them from the System, and created this paradise for them."

"She sounds wonderful," Shari agreed. "To think that one woman could do all that. And what about the other people we've seen?" she asked, and remembered the good-looking man who had waved at her last night: she wouldn't mind getting to know him a little better!

"'Momma's Little Helpers', Ganymede calls them," said Cruse. "They're people like us – refugees from the System. Apparently, when there's enough of them, Momma Mercy intends to strike a blow against the System – maybe start some sort of democracy movement..."

"That's marvellous!" said Shari. "How many of them are there?"

"Ganymede says a few hundred," Cruse revealed. "And that's what worries me..."

"Worries you? Why?"

"You and I were two of the first people to escape from the System," Cruse said. "Or so we thought."

"Three of us," Shari said. "Kristas was with us as well."

"Kristas, of course..." Cruse said slowly, and frowned. "I'd forgotten about him for a moment... But if hundreds of people had got away from True-heart and his creeps surely we'd have heard something of it?"

126

"The Child Roland," Shari reminded him. "When it comes to propaganda there's no one to beat him."

Cruse paused for a moment. "You're right, Shari," he said. "I'd forgotten about him too..." He raised a hand to his brow.

"You're getting forgetful in your old age!" Shari quipped, and then noticed the red rash on Cruse's hand: it was similar to the one on her own arm.

"It's nothing," Cruse told her. "Must have scratched myself in the night, that's all. I'm still not happy."

Shari sighed, and left her room, closing the door behind her. She walked into the arboretum, and picked a flower and sniffed it; the fragrance sent thrills of delight coursing through her body.

"You're never satisfied," she said. "This place is like a heaven on Earth – trees and flowers, more than enough food to eat, an unpolluted atmosphere, and a haven from the System. What more could you want? It's perfection itself!"

"I don't like perfection, Shari," was Cruse's reply. "It dulls your mind. The Mutes here have got it much too easy –"

"Too easy!" Shari couldn't believe what she was hearing. "You surely don't begrudge them what they've got here in the Honeywell, do you? After all they've suffered on the surface?"

Cruse chose not to reply. "Everyone should experience some form of hardship," he said. "It's only by overcoming hardship that a species can progress." He pointed over to a small arbour where Ganymede was sitting chatting with Barnaby Rudge. "If the System invaded the Honeywell, would Ganymede and his people be able to defend themselves, after being cossetted so much by Momma Mercy?"

"They were ready to defend themselves last night," Shari told him, reminding him of their ambush in the stone circle.

"They didn't fire those laser-rifles, though, did they?" Cruse pointed out. "I'm not altogether sure that they knew how to."

"Or maybe they didn't want to," Shari said, as she and Cruse sat down on a small stone bench overlooking the stream. "Or perhaps they couldn't – like ... like...'

"Like who?" Cruse asked her.

Shari shrugged. "I'm not sure," she said, and raised a hand to her brow. In the back of her mind she could see very faintly the smiling face of a blond-haired young man, but she found that she couldn't remember his name.

"Greetings, my children."

They both turned around to see an old woman watching them. Short and stout, she seemed to be about seventy. She had a mass of thick silvery-white hair, swept back from a face which, though creased with deep lines, was still one of the kindest, most trustworthy faces Shari had ever seen. Her green eyes blazed with a fierce intelligence, and when she smiled she revealed a set of perfectly white teeth, save for one gold tooth in her upper mouth which twinkled in the artificial sunlight. She was dressed like all the other Helpers in the Honeywell in a simple two-piece green tunic. Her only concession to vanity was a ruby brooch.

Shari stood up to greet the old lady, who urged her to resume her place with a wave of her hand; in contrast to the rest of her rather dumpy and homely appearance, her fingers were long and elegant and finely manicured.

"There's no need to get up, my child." Her voice was warm and welcoming, reminding Shari of her grandmother, who had died when she was eleven. "Momma doesn't stand on ceremony here, and neither should you!"

"Momma Mercy?" Shari asked, and the old lady beamed.

"That's right enough!" she chuckled. "Not my real name of course, but my children like to call me by that. I've been known as Momma Mercy for so long now that I don't think I can even remember my own name any more. You forget things in the Honeywell, y'see, things which you don't want to remember..."

"You're in charge here?" asked Cruse.

Momma Mercy nodded. "That's right, Cruse."

"How did you know my name?"

A note of wariness in Cruse's voice, but Momma Mercy merely gave him an even broader smile.

"Ganymede told me," she explained. "You and Shari are quite famous, you know – two of the first ever people to fight the System and successfully evade capture for so long –"

Cruse interrupted Momma again. "What about your 'Little Helpers'?" he demanded.

For a second Momma hesitated. "You and Shari were the first people from Pasiphae to fight the System, I mean," she finally said, keeping her eyes fixed on Cruse. "Momma's Little Helpers have come from other outposts of the System – from Japetus and Titan, TerraNova and even the mines of Uranus."

Shari stared at Cruse, making no secret of her annoyance: here he was giving the third degree to someone who up to now had only seemed to have their best interests at heart! Couldn't he forget his cynicism just for once!

"It's a wonderful place, Momma Mercy," Shari said.

"Please, my precious, call me Momma – everyone else does," she said, and looked around at the budding trees, and then further, up at the ceiling hundreds of metres above their heads from which artificial sunlight beamed, and sparkled off Momma's ruby brooch.

"This place was supposed to be a huge underground citadel for the hierarchs of the System. Of course, then it was decided to leave the Home Planet altogether, and this old place was left abandoned and forgotten, until I came to reclaim it about ten years ago now."

"You escaped the System – someone as old as you?" Cruse asked disbelievingly.

"Cruse! Don't be so rude!"

Momma laughed, a kind, forgiving laugh. "Cruse is right to be suspicious of me," she said. "When the Trueheart was the System's Security Chief, then I worked alongside him in the Scientific Research Corps –"

"I've never heard of you," Shari said, and Momma smiled indulgently.

"Why should you have, my poppet?" she asked pleasantly. "I was but a minor official, a hireling, that's all."

"The Inheritors told me you were one of the top people in System government," Cruse said. There was something about this smiling old lady that jarred with him; his senses seemed to be telling him that there was something not quite right about her.

Momma Mercy tut-tutted. "They do so like to exaggerate," she said. "I was just a mere bio-geneticist..."

"Responsible for the Mutes," Cruse said steelily, and Momma Mercy hung her head in shame.

"In part, yes," she confessed. "But I didn't know the full extent of the Trueheart's plans. I wanted to improve the human form, bring it to its next natural stage of evolution. But the Trueheart wanted to warp my plans, wanted to evolve *homo sapiens* not into *homo superior*, but *homo tyrannicus* – an awful, war-like creature which would help him achieve his aim of seizing total control of the System..."

"That sounds like Trueheart," said Shari.

"And the Mutes –" here Cruse nodded over at Ganymede who was still talking to Barnaby some way off out of earshot – "were the botched results of those experiments to create a superbeing?"

"You know that, Cruse," Momma said. "But believe me when I tell you that I didn't know what was going on. Not until afterwards."

"Now where have I heard an excuse like that before?" he sneered.

There was a sudden angry flash in Momma's eyes, and for a moment Shari half-expected the old lady to lash out at Cruse. Then she seemed to calm down and relax. When Momma spoke again, she was close to tears.

"When I did discover the Trueheart's real intentions, I managed to commandeer a cruiser –"

"Without getting caught," Cruse said. "An old woman like you..."

"Cruse!" Shari reprimanded once again.

"Without getting caught," Momma confirmed, and glared at Cruse, as if defying him to contradict her. "You did as well, Cruse. As a supposedly trustworthy member of the Science Corps I was familiar with all the access codes which would deactivate the Island's security systems. I flew here to the Home Planet, where I now try and help the mutants as best I can – it is the least I can do for all the pains and torments the System has put them through."

"And the System hasn't tried to track you down?" Cruse persisted with his questioning.

"I may be an old woman, Cruse, but I'm not without guile," Momma Mercy said, and smiled superiorly. "I blew up my ship shortly after I landed on the Home Planet, faked my own death. You could have done the same thing if you'd had your wits about you."

Shari grinned. Momma Mercy had scored a point over Cruse and they both knew it.

"And so you came to the Honeywell," Cruse said, changing tack slightly. "And it's from here that you plan to establish a base from which to attack the System at its very heart?"

"Exactly," Momma said. "I was trained as a biologist and a geneticist in order to save and improve life. All the Trueheart wants to do is to twist and pervert it for his own ends." She shuddered. "I hate him – I hate him with every fibre of my being. As do all my Little Helpers. There's nothing I would like more than to see him dead."

Cruse nodded grimly. "You'll have to join the queue," he said, and his eyes misted over with unshed tears. "Ten years ago – about the same time you escaped the System – Trueheart murdered a friend of mine. She was one of the most brilliant students at the Academy on Pasiphae, and he had her slaughtered in front of my eyes."

Momma looked at Cruse, and then at Shari, and then back at Cruse: she had caught the emotion in Cruse's voice and knew that Donovan Trueheart's victim had been more than just a "friend" to Cruse.

"And who was this person, Cruse?" she asked softly.

"It doesn't matter," Cruse said gruffly and stood up to leave. Shari reached out for him and held his arm.

"It helps to talk, Cruse," she said sympathetically. "I'm sure Momma would want to hear about how much you loved Marla..."

Momma Mercy smiled, like an elderly aunt supervising two squabbling children. "I'm certain that Cruse will tell me in his own good time, won't you, Cruse?" she said, and then frowned. "But let's not dwell on the long-dead. Let's think of the living. Where is the third member of your party?"

"Third member?" asked Shari, somehow not quite understanding what Momma was talking about.

Momma Mercy tut-tutted and shook her head. "Surely you haven't forgotten about that young man, your best friend, so quickly, have you?"

Kristas! Somehow in all the excitement of the past few hours Shari had almost completely forgotten about Kristas and the other Inheritors waiting for them back in London. And there was a small niggling doubt at the back of Shari's mind: how did Momma know about Kristas?

"Momma! We must get back to them!" she said, as all her memories rushed back. "Kristas is ill – he needs our help..."

"Well, we have extensive medical facilities in the Honeywell," Momma told her. "If you'll tell me where he is then I can arrange for some of Momma's Little Helpers to bring him here..."

Cruse stepped forward. "It's OK," he said. "We can take our own skimmer as we intended to."

Before we forget about Kristas, he added to himself. There were times when Kristas irritated Cruse intensely, but he was still a friend, one of the few that Cruse had. And Cruse never forgot about his friends. At least not until now.

"Nonsense," chided Momma. "We have much faster transportation than your skimmer." She turned back to Shari. "Now where is your friend?"

"In London, Momma," Shari said, before Cruse could stop her. "In the tubes that used to be the city's underground railway system." She closed her eyes and tried to recall the name of the station Muhajji had taken them to. "King's-Cross-Saint-Pancras," she repeated from memory.

Momma clapped her hands, in some sort of triumphant gesture, and grinned. "Excellent!" she said. "So the old tube lines still exist, do they? I'd've thought they would have been destroyed by now. Momma will talk to her Little Helpers and we will have your friend safe and well with us in no time!"

"But. . ." Cruse began, but Momma silenced him with a wagging finger.

"But me no buts, young man!" she chided. "Momma knows best! Just you wait and see." And with that Momma Mercy stumped off along the pathway through the trees.

When she had gone, Cruse turned angrily to Shari.

"You little idiot!" he said. "Why did you tell her where Kristas and the others are?"

Shari pouted. "What harm can it do?"

Cruse watched the departing figure of Momma Mercy. "None, I hope," he said. "But why do I get the feeling that there's something very nasty brewing here in Paradise?"

Pasiphae, one of the satellites of mighty Jupiter, spun on its axis, its two million inhabitants blissfully ignorant of the battleship which orbited it, cloaked in a shield of invisibility which deflected all light.

Pasiphae had been one of the pioneer worlds, when men had first ventured out past the Asteroid Belt to mine the gas giants of Jupiter and Saturn, and, as such, it held a special place in the hearts of the people of the System. But Jupiter had now been mined almost to exhaustion, and Pasiphae's profitability was decreasing year by year. Pasiphae had, in fact, served the purpose for which it had been terraformed and colonized, and now it was to serve a further, more secret and more evil purpose.

On the bridge of the battlecruiser, Commander Schreck regarded the yellow-green world displayed on his scanner. Accompanying him on the bridge were about ten hand-picked men and women, all of them unable to speak, and whose loyalty to him and the System was without question. Such loyalty was essential for the task they were about to carry out; nevertheless, after their mission was completed and they had all returned to the Island, they would be summarily executed. As the Child Roland was always saying, it didn't pay to have too many people knowing too many secrets.

A light buzzed on Commander Schreck's control panel, and he activated a secondary scanner control. The holographic image of the Child Roland presented itself to him, hovering above the small circular projector built into the control deck.

"Is everything in order, Commander?" asked Roland's disembodied voice.

"Merely waiting for your command, sir," Schreck replied.

The Child Roland smiled. "You are an intelligent and self-willed man, Commander," he said. "I wouldn't presume to give commands to a man of your stature. I am sure you will do your duty when you imagine the time to be right... And after you have done your duty, you are required elsewhere..."

And then the Child Roland's image faded from view.

Schreck smirked. The Child Roland was a wily one, and that was no mistake, he concluded. He had given no command, had not even mentioned the purpose of their mission, presumably in the highly unlikely event that someone had tapped into their sub-etheric communications channel. Roland would go far, perhaps as far as the Presidency itself.

"OK, lads," Commander Schreck said to his crewmen. "There's no time like the present, is there? Let 'em drop."

Ten pairs of hands operated five different sets of launching commands, punching in the secret codes which would engage the bombs which the battle-cruiser carried in its belly.

There was a whirring of mechanisms, and slowly the underside of the ship opened to reveal five stubby torpedoes. At this command from Schreck, the missiles were launched, hurtling down into Pasiphae's atmosphere.

Schreck barked another command, and the ship engaged its sub-tachyon drive, and sped away from the planetoid at approximately one twentieth of the speed of light.

When Pasiphae exploded in a brilliant cloud of

nuclear energy, Commander Schreck was already halfway back to Mars.

Millions of klicks away, in the tubes underneath the ruins of London, Kristas woke up – and screamed and screamed and screamed. It felt as though the fires that rained on Pasiphae were raging throughout his entire body, and he seemed to feel the uncomprehending agonies experienced by every man, woman and child on the planet, as their blood turned to vapour, their eyes to molten tissue, and their limbs to ashes.

He smashed his fists against his head, as if that could drive out all the torments he was suffering, and leapt out of bed. Scarcely knowing where he was – or indeed who he was, as two million screaming souls seemed to be struggling to gain occupancy of his mind – he staggered out of the room, along winding corridors, and up long-dead escalators, and finally up into what used to be the circular booking hall of the station known to twentieth- and twenty-first century Londoners as King's Cross Saint Pancras Underground station.

Alice, who had been sleeping in the next room, and who had been awoken by Kristas's screams of anguish, chased after him, up through the booking office, and out into the mist-enshrouded ruins of what once had been the greatest city on the face of the planet.

Exactly six minutes and twenty-seven seconds after

Pasiphae had been destroyed by Schreck's five bombs, all entertainment programmes on the two hundred and fourteen channels of System Broadcasting were interrupted.

In addition, every smart-box in the entire System activated itself, or interrupted the program it was running, for a message from the System President.

The tear-stained face of Donovan Trueheart appeared, his eyes red with what seemed like grief (but which was actually the result of an extremely potent bottle of wine provided for him by the Child Roland), and his hair dishevelled as if he had just been dragged out of bed by a piece of particularly bad news. The camera shot pulled back to show Gabriel sitting on his lap, being stroked by his master: it was the perfect picture of a friendly and benign ruler of the System.

"My friends," the Trueheart began and a billion hearts across the System leapt for pity, as his voice cracked, and tears began to roll down his ruddy cheeks.

"My friends," he started again, "today is a black day in our glorious thousand-year-old System. Today we have lost the two million souls of the planet Pasiphae – '

The news broadcast cut to a slow-motion picture of the exploding planetoid, taken, so the Trueheart claimed, by one of that world's orbiting weather satellites (no one thought to ask how such a defen-

140

celess piece of hardware could have escaped the conflagration).

"I realise that times are indeed hard – no one knows more than me when I go without food and drink so that there may be more for you, the people whom I am privileged to serve. But I ask you all – nay, I beseech you all from the bottom of my True Heart – to rally round me in this moment of crisis, to support me, to follow me.

"Let us forget our petty differences, let us unite as one people, one System, under one leader, until we track down and destroy the vile perpetrators of this most iniquitous deed. Commander Schreck, one of my most trusted lieutenants, is already on their trail and I can assure you that the murderers will be brought to trial as quickly as possible."

On the Child Roland's orders, the camera went in for a close-up of the Trueheart's grief-stricken face.

"Trust me, my people. Let there be no more quarrelling amongst ourselves, let us make the traitors pay for the deaths of all those men, women – and those poor, poor innocent children – slaughtered today on our own dear departed world of Pasiphae.

"Let us unite in our pursuit of these vile assassins. Let there be but one people, one System, one Trueheart!"

And then the Trueheart broke down, live on camera, in tears of despair and sorrow and regret for the senseless slaughter of almost two million people.

And the most frightening thing was that everyone
believed him.

The Call of the Wild

"Kristas? Kristas? Where are you?" Alice called out, trying to see through the dense shroud of fog which hung over this part of London. She coughed: it had been a long time since she had ventured out on to the surface for this length of time, and she had forgotten just how toxic the mists could be.

There was no reply, just the far away howling of the wolves, as they embarked on their nocturnal quest for food. Hugging herself for warmth, Alice closed her eyes, trying to intuit Kristas's location, and she stumbled off through the rubble in search of him, her eyes constantly darting around her for sign of any approaching predator.

She walked, called out Kristas's name for what

seemed like hours, but which was in reality little more than five minutes, when she heard a mournful whimpering coming from somewhere above her. She was standing at the foot of a pile of rubble, and she looked up to see Kristas, silhouetted against the orb of the full moon. He was curled up in the foetal position, sobbing softly to himself.

Alice scrambled up the heap of stone, and reddened bricks, and steel pylons, to join him. Casterbridge had once told her that this rubble was all that remained of one of London's greatest buildings: a massive library that stretched over several square klicks, the depository of all knowledge on the planet, so they said. But the books and disks and programs which it had once stored had now all vanished – burnt or melted in the fire-storms of the Great Colonial War.

When she reached the top, she took Kristas in her arms, and ran her fingers through his hair. He reached out for her, and held her fast, like a baby clutching his mother. Only a few hours ago, Alice and all the other Inheritors were relying on Kristas and his friends for help; now the situation was reversed.

"They're all dead, Alice," Kristas moaned. "All my friends, all my family back home on Pasiphae – they're nothing more than two million cinders floating around in space. I saw it, Alice, I felt it in my mind..."

"Hush, now," Alice crooned. "There's nothing you can do about it. . ."

"What's happening to me, Alice?" Kristas sobbed.

"You're telepathic, Kristas, we know that," Alice said. "More sensitive to psychic vibrations than most of us. . . That's why you can sense danger before it happens, and find your way through country you've never crossed before."

"But the Inheritors are telepathic too," Kristas said. "And none of you is suffering like me. . ."

Alice shook her head. "We're mildly telepathic – we had to evolve and develop that part of our brains just to keep ourselves alive in the Wastes," she said. "But you . . . you're different. . .' A sudden thought struck her. "How long have you been having these headaches?"

"About three months," Kristas said. "Maybe four. . ."

"And the nightmares you told me about?"

"The same," Kristas said. "You think they're connected?"

Alice nodded. "It was something you told me about earlier – you called it the Other. . ."

Kristas nodded, and urged her to continue.

"It started me thinking," Alice said. "It reminded me of something which happened a long time ago. I was just a kid at the time, so I'd forgotten about it until you mentioned it. A girl about your age, one of the Inheritors, started having headaches and nightmares, just like you. I remember the grown-ups telling me to stay away from her. They said she could see into other people's minds, know what they were thinking. In the end it drove her mad, and she ran on to the surface too. We found her body a few days later – or rather what was left of it. She'd been eaten by the wolves... But as she ran out of the tubes she was screaming that she had to find something, find someone. It was asking for her, you see, and she couldn't ignore its call..."

"Did this something have a name?' Kristas asked, even though he already knew the answer.

"The Other," Alice said. "The Other was calling out for her – just as it's calling out for you..."

"I'm scared, Alice," Kristas said.

"Don't be,' she reassured him. "That girl was all alone; I'm with you now..." She listened; the sound of the wolves was closer now. "Are you strong enough to walk?" she asked.

Kristas nodded, and Alice helped him to stagger to his feet. Suddenly the whole area was bathed in an icy-blue light. Alice pulled him back down to the ground.

"System troopers!" she whispered as they both watched the dreaded shape of a hunter-ship descend from the night sky and land in the ruins of what had once been King's Cross railway station. A hatchway opened, and Schreck and a dozen jackbooted

StormTroopers, disembarked, their laser-rifles primed and ready for action.

"What are they doing here?" Kristas asked.

"Keep your head down!" Alice urged. "They can't see us up here!"

"They're after the Inheritance!" Kristas gasped, but Alice reminded him that the legendary source of power was safe with Shari and Cruse in the Honeywell. She watched with dread as she saw Schreck and his henchmen break open the hatchway which the Inheritors used to enter and leave their underground sanctuary.

"Trueheart's sent them to capture us!" Alice said with dread. "But how could they know where to find us? We've remained hidden from them for hundreds of years! As far as they knew, all the tubes were destroyed long ago in the Colonial War!"

Schreck's men remained in the tubes for about an hour, while Kristas and Alice stayed hidden amidst the rubble, hardly daring to think what might be happening beneath their feet. When they finally left, Schreck was clearly annoyed; even though Kristas and Alice were about fifteen metres away from him, they could still hear his voice as he berated his troops.

"There will be hell to pay for this!" he roared. "The Magnificence will not be pleased. We must find him – find him before it is too late!"

One of the StormTroopers said something to Schreck which they couldn't quite catch.

"Leave them," Schreck barked back. "I'll send a skimmer to clear up the mess later! Now let's get as far away from here as we can before this blasted fog chokes us all to death!"

Schreck turned and marched into the hunter-ship, followed by his men. Within minutes the ship had taken off and vanished into the darkness.

Kristas and Alice stood up, left their hiding place, and walked slowly back to King's Cross, and the entrance to the tubes. With a heavy heart they descended. What they found sickened them.

In every tunnel, in every antechamber, on every platform, it was the same: bodies piled on top of each other, and blood spattering the white-tiled walls of the Inheritors' home. Everywhere there was the vile and bitter stench of death: Schreck had slaughtered every single one of the Inheritors living in the tubes.

"This is my fault," Kristas said. "Those Storm-Troopers came here to find me..."

"They would have killed them whether they knew you were here or not," said Alice. "Once they discovered where we were hiding..."

"But how could they have known?"

Alice averted her face from the sight of the massacre, otherwise she knew that she would throw up. She began to walk towards the exit, tears streaming down her face. Kristas ran after her.

"Where are you going?" he asked her.

"Out of here," she said, her voice strangely steady.

"You heard what that Trooper said – they're sending someone back here to 'clear up the mess' – whatever that means. . ."

Kristas chose to remain silent, remembering what Cruse had told Shari about the fate of some of the mutants, and about the starving System's predilection for human flesh.

"But where to?" he asked. "We won't stand a chance on the surface – with the wolves and the mists and the System's hunter-ships patrolling the skies."

"We'll have to risk it," Alice said. "Find somewhere to hide out, until the Troopers have been and gone. Then we can return to the tubes. Perhaps some of the Inheritors escaped after all. . . Do you think you're up to it?"

Kristas nodded; his legs were still shaky, but his headache had ceased for the moment, and his temperature was back down to normal, for the time being at least.

"We can't stay here, in London," he said.

"We have to," Alice protested. "We have to wait for Cruse and Shari to return!"

"I told you before – they won't return," Kristas reminded her.

"How can you be so sure?"

"I'm sure, that's all. Trust me, Alice, there's only one place we can be safe now. . ."

"The Honeywell? But that's too far away. It could

take us weeks to get there on foot without a skimmer."

"Then we'd better start right away, hadn't we?" Kristas snapped back. "I remember Shari saying that there might still be old supply depots on the other side of the river. We might be able to find some abandoned vehicle that's still serviceable."

Alice considered the matter. "The bridges across the river have all been destroyed," she reminded him. "But some of the tubes pass under it. If we are quick we could reach the south side before those StormTroopers come again."

"Then it's settled," Kristas said. "We take oxymasks and whatever supplies we can find from the tubes, and set off."

"Barnaby took our only map," Alice pointed out reasonably. "We've no idea how to find the Plain of Stones, and the Honeywell, when we do get there!"

Kristas smiled at Alice and a curious shudder ran through her body. There was a strange gleam in Kristas's eyes now – nothing frightening or threatening, but something different, something almost alien. It was as though she was seeing Kristas for the first time. Alice felt like a little girl again, gazing up into the eyes of an old, old man from a far distant land. And then the look was gone and Kristas was his normal self again.

"I know how to get there,' he said with absolute certainty.

150

"But how?"

"Because the Other is waiting for me there," Kristas said. "The Other will guide us to him... He is waiting for me ... for both of us..."

"But what do we do when we get there?" Alice asked, and Kristas shrugged.

"I don't know," he admitted. "Perhaps the Other will tell me. All I know is that I have to be with him."

Like walkers in a dream, Kristas and Alice turned and headed back towards the tubes. There was a long journey ahead of them, and at the end of it they only knew that the Other was waiting for them, patiently expecting them as a parent would long-lost wayward children.

Or as a starving spider would, waiting in its gossamer parlour for an unwary fly.

The Honeywell

Life is good, decided Shari, as she walked, arm in arm, with Barnaby, in the wooded glades which lay at the centre of the Honeywell. In the trees, birds twittered happily to each other, and fish leapt and dived in the streams which trickled through the woodland, tinkling like the sound of so many bells.

They stopped and Barnaby plucked a flower from a nearby bush, raising it to Shari's nose for her to smell: its fragrance was lush and heavy. Even the air itself was sweet, laden with the heady scent of roses. *Momma Mercy gives me all I need and I love my Momma*, Shari thought happily.

"You've hurt yourself, Barnaby," she said, glancing at his bare, muscular arm. There was a red rash just below his elbow, near his arterial vein.

"Probably scratched myself, that's all," Barnaby said indifferently.

"Just like me then," said Shari, and, when Barnaby expressed his concern, reassured him: "It was nothing; it happened –" she paused and frowned – "oh, I don't know, a long time ago. I lose track of the days down here in the Honeywell. It seems like ages since I've seen Casterbridge, for example."

Now it was Barnaby's turn to frown. "Casterbridge? Who's he? Some new friend of yours?"

Shari giggled. "Don't be silly," she said. "You know who Casterbridge is, he's ... he's..." Shari frowned. "You know, *I've* forgotten who he is!" She yawned. "He couldn't have been all that important, after all then, could he?"

"Perhaps Muhajji will know?" Barnaby suggested.

"Muhajji!" scoffed Shari. "We hardly see him these days! He spends so much time with Momma!"

"The System has to be fought, Shari," Barnaby reminded her. "Momma says she needs him."

"And not me or Cruse!" Shari sounded most put out. "Maybe I should go and look for Momma and tell her what I feel. I want to help her in the fight against the Trueheart."

"Not now, Shari – Momma is tired," Barnaby reminded her. "She's gone to the Upper Rooms to rest and you know that we're not allowed up there when Momma is taking one of her little naps."

Shari sulked. "I suppose not," she said. "Anyway,

I'm sure her Little Helpers will be of more use to her than we are."

They turned a corner, and saw Cruse, sitting on a bench tossing pebbles into the water of a stream. He gave them a nod of welcome, and they joined him on the bench.

Shari kissed him on his cheek: he was clean-shaven, his long black hair was freshly washed, and he was no longer wearing his combat fatigues, but the same green tunic as Shari and Barnaby. He shook hands with Barnaby.

"Cruse, are you OK?" Shari asked, her voice full of concern. "You look so tired."

Cruse shrugged. "Couldn't sleep," he said.

"Bad dreams?" Barnaby asked sympathetically. "You should talk to Momma about those. When I was having those nightmares last week she gave me some drugs to take. Now I've never felt better!"

Cruse looked at Shari. "They were just so vivid. All about you and me..."

Shari giggled again. "Cruse, you should be ashamed of yourself!"

Cruse ignored her good-natured teasing. "There was someone else in the dream too. Someone I met in a place called Pasiphae."

"Pasiphae? Where's that?" asked Shari, who had been born on that planetoid twenty years ago, and who was still unaware of its destruction on the orders of Donovan Trueheart.

"One of the System worlds, I think," Cruse said. "Although it's hard to remember these days. But this guy seemed so familiar. Tall, blond. He said his name was Kristas, Kristas Chernenko."

Shari laughed. "Never heard of him!" she said.

"Have you spoken to Momma about this, Cruse?" Barnaby asked.

"Of course," was the reply. "She was very worried. She gave me some drugs to help me sleep."

"And they didn't work?" Shari was now worried; when Momma's drugs didn't work then something was seriously wrong.

"There were other people in my dreams too, Shari," Cruse continued. "Someone called Jarrl – he said he was your father. And a robot called Kilimanjaro –"

"Kili..." said Shari, as a long-forgotten memory struggled to surface. She shook he head.

"And an old man called Casterbridge..."

Casterbridge.

Shari and Barnaby exchanged worried looks.

"I've thought of Casterbridge, too," Shari revealed to him. "Who is he?"

"How the hell am I supposed to know!" Cruse blasted out, and Shari was taken aback: here in the Honeywell Cruse was normally so calm, so placid. She could never imagine him being capable of anger. "That's what's so bad about these dreams, that I don't know what they mean. They're like memories I've forgotten, taunting me, teasing me to remember them."

"All of us had a hard time, before Momma rescued us from the System, and gave us sanctuary," Barnaby said sympathetically. "It's bound to have affected some of us more than others..."

"*I can't remember*, damn you!" Cruse snapped. "I can't remember who Kristas is or who Casterbridge is, or anyone else! All I know is that I escaped from the System when Marla was killed and then..."

"Yes, Cruse?" Shari encouraged him.

"And then the rest is a blank until Momma welcomed us to the Honeywell," Cruse said, close to despair.

Shari stood up. "You're not feeling well, Cruse," she said. "I'm off to get you help. Momma will know what to do."

"Shari, you can't disturb her now!" Barnaby protested.

"Cruse is my friend, Barnaby – Momma will understand," said Shari, and ran off to the elevators which would take her to Momma in the Upper Rooms. As she went, Barnaby watched her admiringly.

"She certainly has some spirit," he remarked to Cruse.

"She used to be so different," Cruse chuckled fondly. "When we first met she was so naïve and unconfident. Both she and Kristas were."

"Kristas again?"

Cruse smiled weakly and shook his head. "I'm sorry, Barnaby," he said. "It's just my imagination. There's no such person as Kristas and there never has been..."

"Don't worry yourself, Cruse," Barnaby said, and gestured all around them, at the trees and flowers, and, above them, at the seemingly topless towers of the Honeywell. "This is not the place for worries: we have all we want here in the Honeywell. Momma Mercy gives us all we need –"

"– and we love our Momma," concluded Curse, and sighed. For the first time in he didn't know how long – days? weeks? years? – he was no longer sure of anything.

The elevator door slid silently open, and Shari stepped into the Upper Rooms, that level of the Honeywell nearest the surface, entry to which was prohibited to all but Momma Mercy and her Little Helpers.

There were no security checks, no guards to regulate who was granted access to the Rooms, which surprised Shari, but then everyone loved Momma so much that no one would dare go against her wishes. Shari loved Momma too, loved her with all her heart, but Cruse was unhappy, and that was excuse enough to ignore Momma's wishes just this once.

She looked this way and that, unsure which way to

go. The small reception area in which she found herself opened out into a much larger chamber, off which ran several corridors.

This place was much bleaker than the rest of the Honeywell, with large functional pipes running along the length of the corridors; there were no fragrant plants and flowers dotted around, as there were in the other corridors of the Honeywell, and the only sound was not the rushing of small streams or wind chimes, but an all-pervasive humming, the source of which Shari couldn't identify.

Shari suddenly felt dizzy, as for the first time she breathed in the air of the Upper Rooms. It smelt different somehow – sharper, tangier and fresher, although she knew that to be nonsense, because the air of the Honeywell had to be the cleanest air she had ever breathed in her life.

It smelt different from the rose-fragranced air of the rest of the Honeywell in that it had no odour at all. Shari shook her head clear and walked down the corridor, unsure of where to find Momma Mercy. She opened the first door she came to.

The room she entered resembled a hospital ward, with beds lining all the walls, on which unfamiliar bodies rested, hooked up to all manner of tubes and machines. Most of the figures on the beds were unconscious, but several of them silently watched her progress as she padded softly past them.

Not wishing to appear prurient, she regarded them

out of the corner of her eye: they were all mutants, she realized, and decided that Momma must be caring for them until they recovered from the abominations visited upon them by the bio-geneticists of the System. Ganymede was probably here, she told herself, and suddenly realized that she hadn't seen the open-headed mutant for several days now. How could she have forgotten him?

She turned to go: hospital wards made her uncomfortable and had done so ever since she had visited her dying grandmother in one back home on Pasiphae.

Pasiphae. . .

Pasiphae! Now I remember! I was born there!

Shari was suddenly scared: how could she have forgotten her birthplace? But back in the Honeywell she had told Cruse that she had never heard of such a world. What was wrong with her? Was she going mad?

"Shari. . ."

The voice came from behind a curtain near to a door, and Shari pulled it back to reveal a wizened old man lying on a bed, strapped down so that he couldn't move. Drips were attached to the veins in his arms, pumping his body full of chemicals, and a peculiar skull cap was attached to his head, which in turn was connected to a bank of equipment at the side of the bed, registering his brain patterns. Shari moved closer: the old man seemed familiar to her.

"Casterbridge?" she breathed, as her memories came flooding back, and the old man grunted an affirmation.

She looked at some of the other occupants of the beds: not all of them were mutants – some of them were other Inheritors, Inheritors about whose existence she had also completely forgotten.

"What are you all doing here?" she asked Casterbridge. "Why had I forgotten about you?"

"Momma..." Casterbridge gasped.

"Momma Mercy? What's she got to do with all this?" Shari asked.

"Momma needs us, needs the Inheritors," he managed to say.

"Needs you? What for?"

"For the Other..."

"The Other? What do you mean?"

"Save us, Shari ... save our Inheritance..."

"Casterbridge, I don't understand," Shari said, and was about to press the old man for more information, when a door at the far end of the ward opened. Two of Momma's Little Helpers – as brisk and efficient, and as startlingly good-looking as ever – marched into the room. Anxious not to be discovered, Shari darted through the door by Casterbridge's bed.

She found herself in yet another passageway, which led into a huge chamber, almost as large as the remains of Westminster Abbey in which she, Cruse *and Kristas* – now she remembered him! – had sought

160

sanctuary before they had met Muhajji and the Inheritors.

The walls of the chamber were honeycombed with opaque pallets, piled one on top of each other until they reached the ceiling. Shari went up to one of them, stepping carefully over the cables which snaked all around the floor, and tried to look inside.

She could just make out a vague figure inside the pallet – indeed each pallet held a recumbent figure, every one of which was curled up in the foetal position. The cables on the floor seemed to be pumping some manner of blue-green liquid into the pallets for, as she watched, the hazy silhouettes shifted and distorted as though she was looking at something underwater.

"What are you doing here?"

Shari turned to see a young woman, dressed in green overalls, as were all of Momma's Helpers, and who was looking at her curiously. She seemed to be slightly older than Shari, and she guessed that she was about Cruse's age. The woman was carrying a clipboard and she dropped it on a small table as she approached Shari. Shari glanced at the clipboard, trying to decipher the unfamiliar chemical symbols written on it without success. For a moment Shari wondered why she wasn't working on a smart-box and then realized that, if she had been, then the System would have been able to tune into it and track down the Honeywell's location.

"You shouldn't be here at all," the newcomer reproved. "System knows what Momma would say if she found out. And we wouldn't want to upset Momma, would we?"

"Of course not," said Shari, and automatically took a step back from the woman. She was good-looking (of course), with short black hair, a determined chin, and a full and friendly smile, but there was also something alien about her too, something which wasn't quite right, an iciness in her dark eyes. She had a mole, too, just below her left eye, which Shari thought was quite unusual: all of Momma's Helpers usually had flawless skin.

"Don't be frightened," the woman said, and took Shari's arm, gently but firmly. She grinned, like one of Shari's girlfriends might when telling her a salacious piece of gossip. "Tell you what, I won't say anything about this if you won't! Is that a deal?"

"Huh... Yes, OK, it's a deal," agreed Shari, and she allowed the newcomer to lead her out of the chamber.

They walked down a corridor which Shari had never seen before, towards an elevator which she guessed would take her back down to the Honeywell proper. Already Shari could smell the scent of roses on the air, so different to the antiseptically clean air in the ward and the large chamber.

"You're Shari Sharifi, aren't you?" the woman asked.

"That's right," Shari said, "but how do you know my name?"

The woman chuckled. "You're famous around these parts, you and your friends," she said. "Momma loves you very much, you know."

"That's nice to know," Shari said, as the woman waved a hand over the light-sensitive opening mechanism of the elevator door. "But I've never seen you before... What's your name?"

"My name doesn't matter, Shari," she said, and held Shari fast when she stumbled. "Are you all right?"

"Just a little sleepy, that's all," Shari said. The world seemed to be spinning round her and she was starting to wonder where she was.

I will not forget, she repeated to herself. *I will not forget, I will not forget...*

"Let's get you back home to the Honeywell, Shari," the woman said pleasantly. "Everything will be all right then. Everything is always all right in the Honeywell. Momma sees to that."

The Child Roland regarded Donovan Trueheart through dark, appraising eyes, and thoughtfully stroked his beardless chin. Once again, the Trueheart was slumped unconscious and drunken at his desk, a pile of news-disks before him. Roland picked one up, careful not to disturb his master, and inserted it into the tiny slot in the read-only circuit built into the Trueheart's desk.

A series of holograms appeared in the chamber, news reports from all twenty-one – *no*, Roland corrected himself, make that twenty now – all twenty worlds of the System.

The Trueheart's tearful broadcast had had its desired effect: the entire system had been outraged by the destruction of Pasiphae and had rallied around its leader. The traitors responsible for the outrage should be brought to justice, they had all demanded, and it was good that the magnificent Child Roland (whom most of the men respected, and quite a few of the women had a fancy for) was doing so much to hunt them down.

He was only Minister for Information and Enlightenment, they had all said, but the way he was conducting the investigation made him surely worthy of much higher office. The Child Roland smiled: it was good to have the people on his side.

He flicked to another news broadcast. There had been a riot on Rhea, one of the moons of Saturn. For a second the Child Roland was worried: were things no longer going according to plan?

Then he relaxed, and his smile widened. It seemed a group of miners had been suspected of being responsible for the destruction of Pasiphae, and of having planted twin cobalt bombs at the centre of the satellite where they would have done most damage.

Their fellow workers had risen up against them, and killed them. Roland chuckled. If this state of affairs carried on like this he wouldn't have to go to all the bother of finding a scapegoat for Pasiphae's destruction: the people would do his job for him.

Most importantly of all, there were no food riots, no constant worrying about the System's rapidly diminishing energy supplies. And the people loved the Trueheart as they had never loved him before. The Child Roland had performed his duties well. He clicked off the holo-news, and took his smart-box out of the folds of his spotlessly-white tunic.

A familiar face appeared on the smart-box's screen, and Roland gazed adoringly at it. "They love him," he said simply. He glanced over at the Trueheart, who was snoring noisily. "If only they knew the drunken ineffectual fool he has become..."

"Then let their warmest love now be turned to coldest hate," the voice at the other end of the communication link suggested.

"It will be my pleasure," the Child Roland said, and closed down the link.

He walked over to the Trueheart's desk, and clicked a communication switch. There were a few things which the Child Roland needed to clear up first, and, within seconds, Commander Schreck walked into the room. He clicked his heels and saluted the Child Roland; he also stole a surreptitious glance at the drunken form of Donovan Trueheart, and the two empty bottles of wine on the desktop.

The Child Roland sighed. "Alas," he said, "the Trueheart has been working so hard for the good of the System that he's once again fallen asleep at his desk."

"Of course, sir," Schreck said gravely, but not without a sly smile. "We should all be grateful for the Trueheart's selfless dedication to our well-being."

"Indeed," said the Child Roland, and put his arm around Schreck's shoulder in a friendly manner. "That little matter we talked about earlier," he said. "Has it been dealt with?"

Schreck nodded. The ten mute crew members who had accompanied him on his murderous mission to Pasiphae had all been killed.

"Excellent," Roland said. "I knew I could rely on you, Schreck."

Schreck breathed a sigh of relief: he had been worried that the Child Roland had called him into the office to upbraid him about his failure to capture Kristas. Instead, judging by the Child's chummy manner, he wouldn't be at all surprised if he wasn't up for a promotion!

"So there are only three people in the entire System who know about the unfortunate 'accident' on Pasiphae," Roland continued. "The Trueheart, myself and you, Commander Schreck."

Schreck beamed with pride, grateful to be included

in such august company. "You can rely on me, sir," he assured him. "I will not betray you."

The Child Roland smiled his most engaging smile, the smile that had endeared him to all the System. "Of course you won't, my dear and trusted Commander Schreck," he said, hugging him. Then he pulled out of his tunic a dagger which he plunged viciously into Schreck's back. The startled Commander gasped with sheer disbelief, and thudded face-forwards on to the floor, dead.

The Child Roland tut-tutted to himself: some of Schreck's blood had stained his spotlessly white tunic. He knew a zip-gun would have been less messy, but they were so noisy, and the Child Roland had no desire to wake the Trueheart. He needed his sleep, drunken though it might be: it was probably the last nap he'd take in a long, long time.

Roland looked over as Gabriel, who had been resting by the Trueheart's feet, came over and sniffed curiously at Schreck's carcass, and then started lapping at the blood which was oozing out of the wound in his back.

Roland smiled, and patted the lupe on its head: the Trueheart had plainly forgotten to feed him today and the creature was hungry. Gabriel grunted, and continued his feast.

Taking his smart-box out again, the Child Roland tapped out a few commands on its ebony surface. Things were going well for him, even though there had been a few hiccups along the way, not least of all the loss of the boy, Kristas Chernenko. But no matter, he would employ others to search the boy out, and if the Trueheart thought that he was doing it for his benefit, then all the better.

In the meantime, the Child Roland had other work to do. First of all he would have to arrange that all records of Schreck's existence be wiped from the System files, so that his death would never be traced back to him. And then he had an even greater deceit to prepare.

The Child Roland had always been a master of disinformation – or Enlightenment, as he liked to think of it – telling the people of the System the most elaborate lies to ensure that the Trueheart remained in power. The bigger and more outrageous the lie, the Child Roland had always asserted, the more people believed you, and did your will. But now, as long thought-out plans were finally drawing to their conclusion, the Child Roland decided to change his tactics.

Now, he decided, it was time to tell the people the truth.

Not *all* the truth, naturally.

And his own special kind of truth, of course.

I will not forget, I will not forget.

The words echoed and re-echoed through Shari's mind as she talked to Cruse. There was something she

168

wanted to tell him, something she needed to share with him. Cruse would know what to do, Cruse would help her. After all, hadn't he always helped her before, like that time when... Well, she couldn't remember exactly when, but she knew that he had always been there when she needed him.

"You've been dreaming, Shari," Cruse said, as they sat in the arbour, as night began to fall. Rather, there was no night in the Honeywell, but Momma ensured that its internal lighting system dimmed after twelve hours or so, to simulate the change from day into night on the surface.

"I am not dreaming!" Shari insisted, and then began to have doubts. "At least I don't think so... It all seemed so real..."

"You were in the Upper Rooms," Cruse said. "You know that's forbidden..."

"You told me that you were always the one who broke all the rules, way back when Marla was alive," Shari reminded him.

"Maybe I've changed now..." Cruse said. "Momma gives me all I need and I love my Momma..."

Shari shuddered. The words seemed somehow alien, evil even, coming from Cruse's mouth. She remembered other words too, words she had been taught a long time ago.

The System provides and I am content.

Something was not right here, she was sure of that,

but what? She tried to remember the first time she met Cruse; and discovered with a shock that she couldn't.

Cruse had always been here, just as the Honeywell had always been here. They all knew about the surface world, of course, and about the System, but for all they could actually remember of them from personal experience they might as well not have existed.

"I seem to remember a hospital..." Shari said, trying desperately to call up the rapidly fleeting memories. "And a strange room – large, and full of small cells, like the cells in a honeycomb. There were people in them."

Cruse sniggered disbelievingly. "You've imagined it all, Shari," he said. "Only Momma and her Helpers live in the Upper Rooms; everybody knows that. Just be grateful no one found you. We wouldn't want to upset Momma, would we?"

Shari started with shock. Someone else had said those very same words to her.

We wouldn't want to upset Momma, would we?

"There was a girl there!" Shari suddenly remembered. "Tall, about your age. Short, dark hair. But she was different somehow..."

Cruse smiled, but nevertheless decided to humour Shari. "Different? In what way?"

"You know how all Momma's Helpers are so good-looking?"

Cruse chuckled; he'd had his eye on one of Momma's Helpers for a few days now – a sexy

170

blonde. The trouble was, he was too shy to make the first move.

"But this girl was different," Shari continued. "I remember she had a mole just below her left eye."

Cruse's face suddenly paled, and he asked Shari to give him a complete description of the woman she claimed to have met in the Upper Rooms. As she did so, his lips trembled.

"What is it, Cruse?" Shari asked, seeing a pained look come over his face. "What's wrong?"

Cruse shook his head. "Nothing, Shari, nothing," he said, his voice softer than she had ever heard it before. He stood up, and gave her a strained smile. "It was only a dream. That's all it was – just a dream. . ."

The Upper Rooms were in darkness when the elevator door sighed open to allow Cruse access to the forbidden levels of the Honeywell. He glanced around anxiously, but there was no one hidden in the shadows.

He coughed, experiencing, as Shari did before him, the change of atmosphere. Suddenly a whole host of memories came flooding back to him – Kristas, Ganymede, Casterbridge, other Inheritors who had gone missing in the Honeywell, and about whom he'd forgotten.

And one other memory too – a memory that no amount of drugs, or drug-laden air could ever erase completely from his consciousness.

Cruse shook his head, to clear it, and walked smartly forwards through the darkness, following the directions Shari had given him. Within a matter of minutes he was in the huge chamber Shari had described to him, surrounded by honeycombs of cells, in each of which resided the shadow of what seemed to be a human being. The area was bathed in a baleful green light, and the temperature was several degrees higher here than in the rest of the Honeywell.

It's like being in a blasted incubator! he thought to himself, and watched as hundreds of transparent cables pumped vital nutrients into the hundreds of people in the hundreds of cells. He was about to examine one of them more closely when he detected a movement in the shadows.

There was a bank of instruments along one wall, and Cruse could see the back of a woman dressed in green overalls, checking this read-out from the computer, and adjusting that control on another set of instruments. She was suddenly aware of Cruse's presence, and she stopped what she was doing, and turned around, her face still hidden in the shadows.

Cruse made no attempt to hide, but instead walked forward, hoping against all hope, hoping against reason itself. There was an unaccustomed wetness in his eyes, and his legs were trembling as he approached the figure.

"It can't be you," he said, in a trembling and tear-cracked voice. "You're dead. I saw Donovan True-heart shoot you dead over ten years ago..."

"Cruse ... is it really you?" The woman sounded just as astonished as he was.

And then, for the first time in over ten years, Cruse cried, as the woman stepped out of the shadows, and Cruse recognized the short, black hair, the determined chin, the dark eyes, and the mole just below her left eye, which he had always teased her about when they were teenagers.

It was Marla.

Momma's Babies

The sun arose, and Alice smiled fondly at Kristas who was lying beside her in his own separate sleeping bag. His face was bearded now, his hair unwashed, and he no longer looked like the gentle and frail-looking young man she had first met in the tubes almost two weeks ago now. He had regained his strength, as they had moved further away from London, and closer to the Honeywell.

Alice liked to think it was because he was no longer breathing in the toxic fogs that she and her people, but not Kristas, had become accustomed to; but, in her heart of hearts, she knew it was because every day they were getting nearer and nearer to the Honeywell and what was waiting for them there.

Kristas was drawing strength from the Other – who-ever or whatever that was.

They had crossed over a hundred klicks of country, fording streams of noisome chemicals, and climbing hills made up of the rubble and debris the System had left behind when it had deserted its home planet for Mars and the other worlds of the solar system.

Kristas seemed to know where he was going, and after a few days Alice came to trust him. She also learned to heed his instincts when he said that they should hide beneath the crop of an out-hanging rock, or in the ruins of some shattered and long-forgotten building. For sure enough, a few minutes after they had taken cover, a squadron of System hunter-ships would fly overhead; if they had stayed out in the open they would surely have been spotted.

Kristas woke up to see Alice's smile. He returned it, and then, without any further greeting, shuffled himself out of the sleeping bag and stood up, stretching his tired limbs.

"Are you ready?" he asked Alice.

Alice groaned. "The sun's only just come up," she said. "Can't we wait a while?"

"No." His tone was final. "He needs me – without me he cannot be whole. We go on."

And with a weary heart, Alice collected her things,

and followed Kristas, heading westwards towards the Plain of Stones and the Honeywell.

The Magnificent Donovan Trueheart sobbed into his glass of Olympus Mons '92. Before him, on the holo-deck on his desk, was displayed an image of Freedom Fields, one of the central meeting places in New Canberra, the capital city of TerraNova and therefore of the entire System. Masses of demonstrators had gathered there, waving placards and banners, all of which displayed just one word: *Truth*. He swigged another gulp of wine, and looked up at the Child Roland.

"Why do they treat me so badly, Roland?" the Trueheart said, slurring his words. "Why do they want to be told the truth?"

"There have been rumours that you were some-how responsible for the destruction of Pasiphae," the Child Roland reported, his voice carrying no emotion whatsoever.

The Trueheart frowned, and an angry look crossed his face. "You were supposed to spread the infor-mation that the planet's destruction was the work of anti-System terrorists."

"And I did so, Your Magnificence," the Child Roland said. "I even fabricated an entire history for the miscreants; I called their terrorist organization the Dark Tower."

"A nice touch," the Trueheart approved.

176

"I thought it would amuse Your Magnificence," the Child Roland smiled. "What's more, I even persuaded some residents of the Happy Camps on Mars to admit to the deed – in return for their freedom. . ."

The Trueheart arched an eyebrow in interest. "You didn't give it to them?" he asked warily.

"Of course not," the Child Roland smiled. "I had them all shot. On holo-disk, of course: it will serve as a cautionary reminder for all those others who may harbour thoughts against Your Magnificence. I shall run it on all major networks today."

The Trueheart nodded to the holo-image of the demonstrators on Mars. "This isn't being broadcast, is it?" he asked, and Roland shook his head.

"I've ordered a complete black-out on all news programmes," he informed the Trueheart. "We're running a programme about all Your Magnificence's achievements for the System instead."

"Excellent," said the Trueheart and poured himself another glass of wine. "How did these demonstrators find out the truth – I mean, this scurrilous lie about me?"

"Idle gossip and speculation among some of the StormTroopers who knew Commander Schreck before he died," the Child Roland lied. "It seems that he wasn't to be trusted quite as much as we believed."

"So not even my guards are to be relied upon," the

Trueheart said, his eyes brimming over with genuine tears. "I thought they loved me..."

"And most of them do," the Child Roland reassured his master. "Most of them do not believe these wicked untruths about Your Magnificence."

"But they have no proof?" the Trueheart asked.

"None as yet," the Child Roland said, and affected a look of embarrassment.

"What do you mean? Not as yet?"

The Trueheart clutched urgently at Roland's white tunic; with a well-concealed look of disgust, Roland noticed that the Trueheart hadn't cleaned his fingernails for some time.

"Unfortunately, the flight recorder of Schreck's ship has gone missing..."

"What!"

"It seems that Schreck removed it, possibly with the intention of blackmail," the Child Roland said. "I have had his apartments searched, of course, and several of his colleagues have been questioned discreetly. But there is no sign of it ... and if someone gets hold of it..."

The Trueheart's face, ruddied by wine, suddenly paled. The flight recorder contained all the details of the craft's journeys since its construction – including the fact that it had been in the vicinity of Pasiphae when the planet was destroyed. The evidence was circumstantial, but it would be enough to turn most of the System against him.

"We must find the recorder!" the Trueheart ordered. "We must not allow the information it contains to be leaked out to the System*"

"Of course not, Your Magnificence," the Child Roland said. "If it fell into the wrong hands... Well, I would not like to think of the consequences..."

However, despite what he said, the Child Roland did think of the consequences, and liked what he thought: Donovan Trueheart would be exposed for the murderous, drunken tyrant he really was.

Other revelations would surely follow (he'd make sure of that) and the System under the Trueheart would be finally revealed as the corrupt, self-perpetuating elite it always had been. The people, hungry, discontented and betrayed, would demand vengeance, and look to a new leader, one who would put food in their bellies, and warmth into their hearts once more.

There was nothing the Child Roland liked more than making people happy, and, as he excused himself from the Trueheart's presence, he took something out of the pocket of his tunic.

There, nestling in the palm of his hand, was a small, wafer-thin plastic card: the flight recorder of Commander Schreck's ship.

With a spring in his step, and a twinkle in his eye, the Child Roland walked off to his apartments. There was still much to do, before the goal to which he had been aspiring for ten years would finally be reached.

Cruse held Marla in his arms, pressing her close against him, tasting her lips, nuzzling his head in her soft dark hair. After ten years of repressing and holding back his emotions, Cruse was finally expressing the love he had refused to acknowledge for a whole decade.

"I don't understand," he said. "You were dead. I saw you shot down."

Marla released herself (with difficulty and some reluctance) from Cruse's embrace. "The Trueheart shot me down, that's true," she said. "He left me for dead: but I was still alive – just. But I would have been dead if not for Momma Mercy..."

"Momma?"

"It was about that time that she discovered just how evil the System was," Marla said. "She found me, and healed my wounds, and brought me here to the Honeywell."

"But why didn't you come looking for me?" Cruse asked.

"I thought you were dead at first," she said. "And when I learned that you were alive I couldn't find any trace of you."

"I planned it that way," Cruse said. "I wanted to escape the System entirely... But if I'd known that you were still alive..."

180

"We're back together now, that's all that matters," said Marla, and kissed him on the lips.

Cruse smiled. "I suppose I ought to apologize to Shari," he said. "She'd told me she'd been here and I said she was imagining things."

"And who is Shari?" Marla teased. "Your girlfriend?"

"Of course not," he replied, slightly irritated that Marla would even have suspected such a thing. "You know there's only ever been you..." He looked around the chamber, at the honeycombed pods which lined the wall, and the shadowy figures which lay within them. "What is this place, Marla?" he asked. "What are inside those pods?"

A brief frown crossed Marla's brow, and then she took Cruse's arm, and led him out of the chamber. "Let's not talk about that now," she said. "It's a little secret of Momma's..."

"Marla, just what is going on here?" he asked her, once they were out in the corridor. "What is the Honeywell for?"

"What is it for?" Marla repeated. "As a sanctuary from the System, and as Momma's base for her final attack against our oppressors, the hated System and the Trueheart especially."

"That's what I've been told," Cruse admitted. "But Momma still hasn't told me her exact plans. And all I've seen are Momma's Helpers and the mutants she's caring for. I've seen no armed guards, no soldiers –"

"You don't always win battles with guns," Marla said enigmatically.

"And why is the air so different here in the Upper Rooms?" Cruse asked, and for a second he felt Marla freeze.

"Different? What do you mean?"

"In the Honeywell the air is heavy and sweet," Cruse said. "It makes us forget things, makes us forget people..."

"Oh that!" said Marla, as though it was the most natural thing in the world. "A gift from Momma. She fragrances the air so that we forget all those painful things in our past, things which can only ever make us unhappy. Momma thinks only of our welfare, you know." She led Cruse back to the elevators. "Some people are more susceptible to it than others, of course. You were able to resist much of its effects..."

"And the hospital ward?" Cruse was persistent. "Shari said she saw that too. Was she meant to forget that as well?"

Marla turned and looked her lover straight in the eye. "Cruse, trust me, like you always used to," she said. "Those Mutes –"

"Mutants," Cruse corrected her, hypocritically.

"Those mutants are there to help Momma, to help all of us," Marla said. "Just as you – and the Inheritors – are here to help us."

"How can we help you, Marla?" Cruse asked, as they entered the elevator, which began its speedy descent down into the main section of the Honeywell. Already the atmosphere was changing, and Cruse once again smelt the fragrance of roses on the air.

"Do you want to see the Trueheart destroyed for good?" she asked, eyeing him archly.

"You know I do," Cruse replied.

"Then help Momma gain the power source to put her plan finally into operation!" There was a strange, almost Messianic gleam in Marla's eyes.

"Power source? Plan?"

"Join us, Cruse. Let us use the Inheritors and make Momma's dreams come true. Imagine it – a source of limitless power, and you can deliver it to us!"

The Inheritance.

Marla fell silent: she realized she had said too much.

"You want the Inheritance?" Cruse asked, and Marla looked surprised for a half-second, before regaining her normal composure. Cruse told her about the Inheritors' sacred artefact, and of how they had left it in the skimmer, near the circle of stones, when they had arrived at the Honeywell (two weeks ago, Marla told him).

"You can get the Inheritance for us?" Marla asked greedily, as the elevator reached ground level, and the door opened out on to the familiar luscious greenery and rose-scented air.

"If you want it," Cruse confirmed. "And if it will help destroy Trueheart."

"Thank you, Cruse," Marla said, and gave him a long, deep and passionate farewell kiss. "Get the Inheritance for Momma, help her to destroy the Trueheart, and she will be eternally grateful to you – although not as grateful as I shall be."

"I love you, Marla," Cruse said, and stepped out of the elevator.

"And I love you too, Cruse," Marla said, as the elevator door slid closed on her. She smiled to herself: Momma's opiate-laden air might not have had its full effects on Cruse, but Marla had found that a little bit of love worked wonders. Human beings were odd like that.

Chuckling, she took a smart-box out of one of her overall pockets and activated a communication link.

"We were right to spare him and his friend, Sharifi," she informed the person at the other end of the link. "He still doesn't suspect a thing, and is ignorant of our real plans ... and what's more, it seems that the Inheritors will provide us with yet another, secondary power source...

"And then the Other will truly live!"

"She can't be Marla!" Shari protested. "You told me Marla died ten years ago."

"She was wounded, not killed," Cruse insisted. "Momma saved her – just as she's saving all of us

184

now. And they need the Inheritance – I promised to get it for them."

"No." This was from Barnaby. "The Inheritance is our most sacred treasure. It must only be used when the time is right."

"And isn't that now?" Cruse demanded. "When Momma has the chance to destroy Donovan Trueheart and all that he stands for?"

"And how's she going to do that?" Shari demanded.

"Does it matter?"

"As a matter of fact, yes," Shari retorted. "And if the Inheritance – whatever it is – is so important, why can't they go up to the circle of stones and get it for themselves?"

"Quarrelling, my children?" said a familiar voice. They all turned: Momma Mercy had joined them, creeping up on them as silently as a cat might sneak up on a mouse.

"We didn't wish to offend, Momma," Barnaby said, and flushed red with embarrassment. He liked Momma and had no wish to upset her. Indeed Momma was liked equally by all the other Inheritors – all four of them. Barnaby had no memory of the fact that fifteen Inheritors had originally arrived at the Honeywell and that eleven of them, including Casterbridge, had gone missing. Neither, indeed, had Shari or Cruse: Momma's mists of forgetfulness could be very effective.

"And no offence has been taken, Barnaby," said Momma Mercy, and smiled gratefully when offered a seat by him. She eased herself down, complaining about her aching bones exactly like any woman of a certain age would. "The reason why Momma or her Little Helpers cannot go to the surface is that the air up there would make us ill. It's poisoned, polluted by the lies of the Trueheart."

"We survived up there," Barnaby pointed out. "And so did the mutants, and Shari, and Cruse and –" Another name was on the tip of his tongue, but he couldn't quite remember it.

"Of course you did, my poppet," Momma said. "But you and your ancestors have always lived on the surface. Over the years you've evolved an immunity to the atmosphere. People like poor Momma, used to the clean and antiseptic air of the System, would not stand a chance up there."

"The survival of the fittest," said Cruse.

"Precisely, my dear Cruse. And if the poor Mutes – mutants – can live through the experiments conducted on them by the System's bio-engineers, then they can survive anything."

"But what about Cruse and myself?" Shari asked. It was the flaw in Momma's argument, and she knew it. Momma Mercy coughed nervously and then said:

"Who knows, my sweet? Perhaps there was something similar in the atmosphere of Pasiphae. I hear it was a very polluted world."

186

"Pasiphae..."

The name meant something to Shari, and she searched the recesses of her memory, a memory made dull and leaden by Momma's opiates.

Momma looked around, like an old matron, checking to see that no one was eavesdropping on her gossip, before saying: "The Trueheart nuked it, you know, only the other week. At least that's what I've been told. Everyone wiped out in a single flash –" she snapped her fingers – "just like that!"

It was Momma's fatal mistake.

Suddenly all Shari's memories came flooding back.

I will not forget, I will not forget... she had promised herself. But even someone as determined as Shari had been losing her memories little by little, even after they had been returned to her in the antiseptically fresh and clean atmosphere of the Upper Rooms.

Now the shock of hearing that her home world had been destroyed by Donovan Trueheart jarred Shari back to her true senses. The visit to the hospital ward had not been a dream, and neither had been Marla, as Cruse could well testify.

And Kristas had not been a dream either, she realized, with a sudden rush of joy. Where was he now? Was he even still alive? And what was the true purpose of the Honeywell?

Snapped back to reality, Shari checked her grief,

and stilled her tongue from giving voice to the thousands of questions she wanted to ask. "That's terrible, Momma, two million people killed in one fell swoop by Trueheart..."

Momma Mercy patted Shari affectionately on her knee, like a kindly old aunt. "Don't distress yourself, my child," she urged her. "But you do see now why a monster such as he must be stopped, don't you? Why Momma must have the Inheritance?"

Shari nodded. "Yes, of course you're right, Momma," she lied. "I understand now..."

Momma beamed, and raised herself to her feet. "Good! Then everything is as it should be!" She turned to Cruse. "It's nightfall up there on the surface now," she said. "And there are wolves about..."

"And other things too," Shari murmured and reminded all of them of the strange mutated creature they had found inside the circle of stones.

Momma frowned, but pretended not to hear, and continued: "But at first light tomorrow, Cruse, you will return to the skimmer, and bring Momma the Inheritance." She turned to go, heading for one of the elevators, but before she did, she gave Cruse one of her most charming and meaningful smiles. "And I have a message for you, Cruse. Marla is busy now, helping Momma with her little plans, but she told me to tell you that she loves you very much."

Momma Mercy sighed happily as the elevator

ascended to her level. "Momma does so much like happy endings..."

Shari, Cruse, Barnaby and the others had been accommodated in a small settlement of purpose-built huts on the edge of a small wooded glade, and, as the night dragged on, Shari came out of her hut, and crossed over to Cruse's. She rapped on the door, calling out his name. There was no reply. Cautiously, she creaked open the door (there were no locks in the Honeywell; or at least not here).

Cruse was lying on his bed, fast asleep. His face in repose was wiped clean of all its cynicism and suspicion, just as she had been accustomed to seeing it before. Shari smiled to herself, but it was a wry, sad smile and hardly one of joy. In the old days – in the days before the Honeywell – Cruse had been the lightest sleeper of them all; if any intruder had entered his room, as she had just done now, he would have snapped awake and reached for his zip-gun in a flash. Now he had let his defences down, and whether it was the result of his reunion with Marla, or the effect of Momma's doped air, or some combination of the two, Shari wasn't quite sure.

She left Cruse's hut and tiptoed over to Barnaby's hut, and pushed the door open. The Inheritor was snoring softly. Satisfied that no one would spot her leaving, Shari closed the door, and walked through the arboretum towards the elevator, the only witness of her nocturnal excursion a tawny owl sitting in the branches of one of the trees.

It took her a matter of seconds in the high-speed elevator to ascend the thirty-nine levels to the Upper Rooms. Once again she felt her head clearing, as the effects of Momma's air wore off. The change wasn't so pronounced this time, as she had already been successfully fighting off Momma's conditioning ever since the old woman's casual mention of the destruction of her home planet had shocked her back to reality.

The elevator door slid open and Shari stepped out into the Upper Rooms, shrouded, like so much of the Honeywell at "night-time", in darkness. There were still no guards about, and Shari guessed that Momma must be supremely confident of the pacifying effects of the Honeywell's drugged atmosphere. Momma must never have encountered resistance to her plans before, but in the past three years Shari had grown more controlled and self-willed – and it was Cruse who had made her like that.

She recalled Cruse asking awkward questions about the Honeywell, his initial distrust of Momma and the whole set-up; now these questions had stopped, for all that mattered to him in this life was Marla. Marla's sudden reappearance must have seemed like a gift to Momma Mercy, and it was all a little too convenient, Shari decided.

This time Shari didn't enter the "hospital" ward as

she had last time, but walked across the reception area to the door Marla had escorted her through and which she knew led to the huge honeycombed chamber. She activated the light-sensitive panel by the door, and it slid open, allowing her into the chamber beyond.

The honeycombed pods around the chamber were illuminated with the same baleful green glow, which pulsed at regular intervals, and the air was warm, almost unbearably so. It was like being in some giant womb, Shari thought, and she instinctively knew that somehow this chamber held the key to the secret of the Honeywell.

At the far end of the chamber a wide flight of steps led up to a closed door. Curious, Shari approached it, and passed her hand over the door's opening device. It stayed locked. She pressed her ear to the surface of the door – it was made of some strange substance, almost organic in texture – and she listened.

A heartbeat. That was what Shari thought she could hear on the other side of the door. *Drum. Drum. Drum.* A slow, rhythmic pounding, beating once for every three beats of Shari's own heart.

And a sighing, a rasping sound, unbearably sad and strained, as though someone – something – was struggling to find its breath.

Shari shuddered: she was suddenly very scared indeed. She descended back into the main part of the honeycombed chamber, and looked at the figures in the opaque pods. Several of them were moving about, as though alerted by her presence in the chamber. She could hear their fingers clawing and scratching at the inside of the pods, as if trying to break out.

One figure started to pound at its pod, in an attempt to smash the milky-white substance which sealed it in its honeycomb, but the pod was too hard and after a few minutes' fruitless hammering, it gave up and resumed its floating position in the viscous blue-green liquid which Shari imagined filled every pod.

Shari was about to leave the chamber, recognizing that here she wouldn't find any clues as to the Honeywell's true purpose, when she glanced at the desk on which Marla had dropped her clipboard when she had first found her snooping around here. The clipboard was still there; or it may have been another one, for the chemical notations written on it were just as unintelligible to Shari.

However, underneath the clipboard there was a large book, bound in pink satin, a bow stretched into its spine by way of decoration. On the front of the book were printed, in an elaborate cursive script, the words: "Momma's Baby Book".

Shari winced at the cuteness of it all. When she had first come to the Honeywell, Momma's slightly child-like manner had seemed endearing and quaintly archaic, right down to her insistence on recording information not in smart-boxes but on good old-fashioned paper. Now that same manner seemed somehow sinister, and a perversion of everything that had once been good and innocent in the world. Shari opened the "Baby Book" to its middle pages, and gasped as she took in the information on the page which Momma had recorded in her fine flowing script.

"*Baby's Name: Muhajji,*" she read. "*Born: Day 009, System Year 3233.*"

System Year 3233. Surely that was wrong, Shari reasoned. Muhajji was at least twenty years older that her and Cruse, but according to this he was only a youngster of thirteen! She continued reading: "*Psi-abilities: thirty-three per cent.*" This last figure was underlined in red ink, and an exclamation mark had been added next to it. "*Aggression Quotient: Nil.*"

There followed a stream of scientific gobbledegook which Shari didn't understand. Apart from one piece of information, that is, one term which even a schoolkid of five would have recognized: *Deoxyribonucleic acid.*

DNA. The building block of life, the genetic code needed to construct any living organism.

Shari's eyes flicked down to the bottom of the page. Under the entry headed "Baby's Leaving the Nest", Momma had written: "System Year 3244".

Two years ago. Two years ago when the Inheritors had found Muhajji on the banks of the River Thames.

With a terrible sense of foreboding, Shari flipped

through the rest of the book. Each page was similar to the others, with personal details of Momma's "Babies", followed by some chemical and biological notation, and finishing with a note of the year in which they had left the Honeywell. Shari recognized none of the other names.

Except one.

Baby's Name: Marla ("Mad" Marla)
Born: Day 211, System Year 3219
Died: Day 228, System Year 3236

Shari nodded to herself: she recalled Cruse telling her once that Maria had only been seventeen years old when she had been killed by Donovan Trueheart. But why was she of such interest to Momma Mercy?

And then what she read next made Shari's blood run cold.

Born Again: Day 182, System Year 3246

Three days ago.

When Cruse had started doubting the Honeywell.

And suddenly Shari understood everything about Marla, realized what manner of creatures lay within the opaque honeycombed pods, and wondered how she could have been so stupid as not to realize the true nature of Momma's "Little Helpers", with their good-looks, efficient manner, and unblemished complexions.

She felt awe too, at Momma's skills, scarcely able to believe what the old woman had achieved in just three days. If she could do that, what else might she be capable of?

What could she have achieved in ten years?

Yet Shari's new understanding still didn't explain the presence of the mutants and the Inheritors in the hospital ward, the disappearance of Barnaby's people, or the source of the heartbeat beyond the locked door at the other end of the chamber. Shari ripped Marla's page from Momma's Baby Book, replaced the book underneath the clipboard where she had found it, and ran over to the door which she knew led into the "hospital" ward.

It was empty: row upon row of unoccupied beds. She went over to the bed in which she had found Casterbridge. The sheets were rumpled, and the mattress was still warm. The strange skullcap which he had been wearing when she had seen him had been dumped on his bedside table.

Examining the inside of the helmet, Shari discovered tiny electrodes, which, she guessed, would have been used to monitor Caterbridge's brain patterns. *But what was so special about his brain, or indeed those of the other Inheritors?* she asked herself. She recalled that none of the mutants who had also been in the ward had been wearing the helmets.

The survival of the fittest.

The phrase played and replayed itself through Shari's mind. She remembered what Casterbridge had told her and Cruse by the circle of stones; that the

Inheritors had developed their instincts to such an extent that they could almost foresee danger a split-second before it presented itself to them. They had to – if they wanted to survive. Cruse had even suggested that the Inheritors could be mildly telepathic.

She had to go back to Cruse, and tell him her suspicions. Even in his present state, befuddled by Momma's drugs, and confused by Marla's apparent return from the dead, Cruse would know what to do.

But when she returned to the Honeywell, Cruse was nowhere to be found.

Death of a Friend

The sun came up over the circle of stones as it had done for the past five thousand years, washing its grey granite bulk in a reddish-golden glow. Tiny pieces of quartz, embedded in the stones, glittered in the morning light, and any observer would have understood just why the stones had held so much magic for countless generations. Cruse, however, hardly noticed it, just as he hardly noticed the far-distant rumbling in the earth beneath his feet, the source of which, he presumed, to be the vast underground reactors which he knew the Honeywell would need to provide it with power.

His whole attention was focused on the Inheritance, as he dragged the heavy wooden box down the ramp of the skimmer, and towards the huge double-doored entrance to the Honeywell. He still had no idea what great power source the box contained, but Marla had said that she needed it and that was good enough for him. He remembered the old days: Marla had always been the thinker, the one who made all the plans, while he had been the man of action. They had made a good team; perhaps they would again.

For one brief second he remember that moment ten years ago which had changed his life. He recalled the horror on Marla's face, when Trueheart had fired on her, her screams of agony as she fell to the ground, murdered for committing the unthinkable crime of questioning the values of the System. It was hardly credible that someone could have survived an attack like that.

"Cruse, *no*."

Cruse dropped the Inheritance on the ground, and looked up. Shari and Barnaby were standing there, watching him. Barnaby's face was set in a grim expression, but Cruse thought that he had never seen Shari looking so sad before in her life.

"Don't try and stop me, Shari," he said. "Momma wants the Inheritance, and she's going to get it."

"You can't take it, Cruse," said Barnaby.

"And I'm not letting any superstitious claptrap stop me either," Cruse stated, in a voice which brooked no argument.

Shari made a step towards him, and Cruse pulled

his zip-gun out of its holster. He aimed it straight at her.

"Don't make me use it, Shari," he said.

"You'd kill me for Momma?" asked Shari. "Do you really trust her more than you trust me?"

Cruse hesitated, as Shari's words struck home. He searched desperately for something to say. "Momma gives us all we need –"

"I know!" Shari said angrily. "But you were the one who was always suspicious of Momma when we first came to the Honeywell. What's made you so sure now, Cruse?"

"I'm not doing this for Momma anyway," Cruse said. "I'm not even doing it because I think that in some way it'll help us defeat Trueheart. I'm doing it because Marla asked me to do it. . ."

Cruse's voice tailed off, and his gun hand wavered. Shari was right: he had fought off the effects of Momma's honeyed air, and Momma had noticed that. And then Marla had reappeared, and he had acquiesced once more to Momma's demands – demands that were relayed through his lover.

"Marla. . ." Shari's voice was sad and heavy.

"I'm doing this for Marla," Cruse said. "I love her."

Shari shook her head, and for the first time Cruse noticed that she was holding something in her hand. It was a sheet of old-fashioned paper, and she passed it over to him, telling him where she had found it.

With a sinking heart, Cruse read the page ripped from Momma's Baby book.

Baby's Name: Marla ("Mad" Marla)
Born: Day 311, System Year 3219
Died: Day 228, System Year 3236
Born Again: Day 182, System Year 3246

Cruse looked up at Shari and Barnaby. "I don't understand," he said, although a horrible suspicion was beginning to form in his mind.

"Marla is dead, Cruse," Shari said, and walked over and put an arm around his shoulder.

"No!" he exclaimed, and angrily pushed Shari away.

"She died in 3236," Shari said. "The Marla we know now is a clone, grown from the original Marla's cells. So was Muhajji. And that's what all Momma's Helpers are too; that's what the honeycombed room is for — a massive breeding chamber for clones. Momma made Marla purely to ensure your co-operation, although why we're so important to her alive, I don't know..."

"*Nonono,*" Cruse said, and shook his head.

But in his heart of hearts, he knew that Shari was right. He had seen Trueheart shoot Marla dead, aiming a bullet right in the middle of her forehead. How could he have been so stupid to think that Marla could have survived that? Because he loved her, he realized, and he knew that he always would.

His heart broken for the second time in his life,

Cruse fell to the ground, and rested his head on the lid of the unopened Inheritance. Shari came over to him and held him, while the tough and brutal young mercenary sobbed his heart out, no longer caring who saw him in his weakness.

Cruse cried for long minutes, while Shari whispered words of comfort to him, and Barnaby watched on in embarrassment. Up here on the surface, his mind was much clearer, and he remembered Kristas, and Alice, and his fellow Inheritors. He wondered what they were doing now, and was worried when an almost unbearable wave of sadness and foreboding came over him. He felt a terrible emptiness: somehow he knew that he had seen them for the last time.

Finally Cruse stopped weeping, and he looked up at Shari. There was a dangerous gleam in his dark eyes, and, with an involuntary shudder, Shari suddenly realized that Cruse would never cry again in his life.

"Are you all right?" she whispered. Cruse nodded, and bit his lip to stem whatever tears he might have left.

"I'm fine," he reassured her, in a monotone. He glanced over at Barnaby. "First we hide the Inheritance," he commanded. "Momma Mercy shall not get it."

"And then?" asked Barnaby.

"And then we return to the Honeywell," Cruse said. "To kill Momma Mercy."

When Shari, Cruse and Barnaby had left the area, and hidden the Inheritance in a small dry clump of bushes – "What are those red things?" Barnaby had asked when they had found the bushes. "Berries," Shari replied, and started thinking – a skimmer ship, similar to Cruse's, shot out of the sky.

The skimmer was sleek and jet-black, and the latest model, equipped with deadly cannons, sub-tachyon engines and the most sophisticated navigational and defensive capabilities to be found in the System. It hovered for a few seconds over the circle of stones, and then made a horizontal landing a few metres away from the outermost ring. The blast from its engines as it landed was so great that one of the stones was toppled. It had stood proudly in its ring for five thousand years, and now it lay shattered and fallen in the dust and the dirt.

The pilot of the skimmer hadn't even noticed.

Silence followed for a few minutes, broken only by the whirring of unseen instruments which scanned the immediate vicinity, checking for any signs of life. When the skimmer's pilot was sure that he was in no danger, there was a clunking sound of doors being unlocked, and the hatchway slid open.

The first to leave the ship was Gabriel, who scampered down the skimmer's ramp, sniffing and scrabbling in the earth which had been disturbed by the landing. He turned up his snout in disgust — compared to the antiseptic corridors and chambers of the Island, this place stank like some fetid septic tank. The lupe would have turned around and clambered back on board the skimmer, if not for the fact that his master had also disembarked, and was closing the airlock door.

The Magnificent Donovan Trueheart wrapped his heavy scarlet cloak about his portly frame, and shivered. The land stretched out before him, bleak and uninviting, a vision of hell. He felt no guilt or regret in his True Heart, even though the System had been responsible for this devastation; he just felt a kind of disgusted astonishment that people could live in this desolation.

Well, not people exactly, he corrected himself, but mutants and genetic aberrations, and drop-outs like Shari, Cruse and Kristas.

The Trueheart nervously looked all around him, and up in the sky, shielding his eyes from the yellow-red orb of the sun, as if he expected a hunter-ship to swoop down every minute. He instinctively reached for the small mask which covered his mouth. He had heard that the atmosphere on Earth was just about breathable, but he wasn't taking any chances.

Calling Gabriel, who was greedily investigating the rotting carcass of the mutant animal Shari had found in the ring of stones, the Magnificent Donovan

Trueheart began to walk off in the direction of the Honeywell.

Things were going very badly for the Magnificent Donovan Trueheart all of a sudden. And no matter how supportive the Child Roland was back on the Island, right now all that Donovan Trueheart really wanted to do was to go and see his Momma.

The Magnificent Donovan Trueheart was not the only visitor to the Honeywell that day. Shortly after he had disappeared through the great double doors in the hillside, which marked the entrance to Momma Mercy's domain, two other figures appeared on the horizon.

Weary and bedraggled they surveyed the land before them, shading their eyes from the light of the sun. Alice held Kristas's hand as she looked at the circle of stones in the distance.

"They're beautiful," she said, as, like her ancestors before her, she marvelled at the rocks of Stonehenge.

"Sanctuary," whispered Kristas, but he wasn't talking about the Neolithic temple. He directed Alice's attention towards the doors of the Honeywell.

"The Other is there, waiting for me," Kristas said. "Longing for me to make him whole."

"The Honeywell?" asked Alice. Kristas nodded. "But how do we get in?"

"You are our most honoured guests," they heard someone say, and turned around. Five of Momma's cloned Helpers – beautiful, flawless, and all with that strange blank expression in their eyes – had crept up behind them.

"We have been expecting you, Kristas," they said, and Kristas started, wondering how they knew his name. "Momma has been waiting for you for a long, long time. Now will you please come with us?"

Kristas and Alice had no choice but to obey as the cloned Helpers led them to the double doors and down into the Honeywell. Not only was it where Kristas and Alice wanted to go; the laser rifles each of the clones carried proved to be a persuasive argument.

Cruse breathed in deeply of the rose-scented air of the Honeywell. The opiate-laden atmosphere of Momma Mercy's domain had little, if any, effect on him now. Just as its spell over Shari had been broken by the traumatic shock of her learning about the destruction of Pasiphae, so his coming-to-terms with Marla's death had also cleared his own mind.

He sat on a stone bench in the glade, alone. Suddenly there was a noise behind him, a rustling of leaves, and he was aware of someone creeping up behind him. He felt hands on his shoulders, which slowly started to massage the back of his neck.

"You're so tense," came a familiar voice, a voice which Cruse didn't know whether he loved or hated. "You're all coiled up, like a spring ready to snap."

Cruse stood up and turned around. Marla was

standing there, as beautiful and as sexy and as loving as she had always been. She gave him an enchanting smile.

Shari was wrong, Cruse told himself. *Marla is real, and not some twisted and perverted clone, bred by Momma to ensure my co-operation.*

And I love her, I love her with all my heart...

"I've missed you, darling," Marla said, and there seemed to be no way to mistake the sincerity in her voice.

"And I've missed you too," Cruse said.

Marla smiled. "You've brought the Inheritance?" she asked. When Cruse shook his head, Marla frowned. "Momma will be most displeased. Why haven't you brought it?" she snapped.

"Because I... Because I..." Cruse didn't know what to say; how could he tell Marla that he had doubted her, and had believed that she wasn't who she had claimed to be? Like some recalcitrant schoolboy, he shrugged and rammed both his hands into his pockets.

His fingers touched on the piece of paper which Shari had torn out of Momma's Baby Book and given to him.

Baby's Name: Marla ("Mad" Marla)
Born: Day 311, System Year 3219
Died: Day 228, System Year 3236
Born Again: Day 182, System Year 3246

"Is there anything wrong, Cruse?" Marla asked.

206

Cruse shook his head. "I was just thinking, that's all," he said.

"Thinking?" Marla laughed, a sound as clear and as light as a bell. "There's no need to do that in the Honeywell! What were you thinking about?"

"That time we spent together sneaking off school and spent a weekend watching the lupe races –"

"And how Jarrl, our teacher found us there, but couldn't say anything because he'd taken a sick-day to go himself!" Marla remembered. "I remember it well."

Cruse smiled. Shari couldn't be right: could even a genius such as Momma Mercy create a clone which had all the memories of its host?

Died: Day 228, System Year 3236

Born Again: Day 182, System Year 3246

"And remember that time when we went joyriding in a skimmer to Titan and spent five days in the Pleasure gardens there? And how Anya and Corin arranged a surprise party for your sixteenth birth-day?"

"How could I forget?" Marla said. "That party was one of the happiest days of my life."

"But it didn't happen, Marla," Cruse said. "The party didn't happen, and neither of us has ever been to Titan."

"Of course, how silly of me," Marla said. "I must have forgotten..."

"There was nothing to remember in the first

place," Cruse said, as he steeled himself to do what he had to.

Died: Day 228, System Year 3236

Born Again: Day 182, System Year 3246

He whipped his zip-gun out of its holster, and fired at Marla, aiming for the centre of her forehead, just as Trueheart had done with the real Marla, ten years ago. Marla gave an astonished gulp of surprise and fell forwards into Cruse's arms.

They stayed like that for a second, a final embrace, until Cruse pushed Marla off him. She was already cold and stiff by the time she hit the ground. Cruse didn't bother to wipe the blood off his clothes.

He looked to the bushes, from where Shari and Barnaby had been watching everything. Barnaby came up to him and patted him on the back.

"That was a brave thing to do, Cruse," he said. "I know what it must have cost you."

"We're equal now, me and Trueheart," Cruse said grimly, his voice choking but his dark eyes dry and tearless. "We've both killed Marla."

Cruse had attached a utility pouch on to his belt, and he opened it and took out a zip-gun which he tossed over to Barnaby who caught it, and looked at it quizzically.

"What good is this?" he asked.

"To defend yourself, of course!" Cruse snarled. "Maybe shoot a few of that witch's blasted Little Helpers on the way."

Barnaby shook his head. "It won't be of any use," he complained.

"It's easy to operate," Shari said. "I don't like using them either, but if we want to find the Inheritors and the mutants, then we might have to."

"You don't understand," Barnaby said. "I couldn't use it – my fingers wouldn't even be able to squeeze the trigger."

"What do you mean?" she asked.

"Some years ago, back in the Wastes, some friends and I were ambushed by a small band of Storm-Troopers," he explained. "We escaped, but not before taking two of their plasma-rifles."

"I wish I'd known about them when I was in the tubes," Cruse said.

"None of us could operate them," Barnaby said. "It's impossible for us to kill another human being, even to save ourselves." He chuckled wryly. "You could even say that we're genetically programmed not to take another's life..."

"'Genetically programmed'?" Cruse scoffed. "What the System is that supposed to mean? Genetically programmed by who?"

"By Nature?" suggested Shari. "There are so few Inheritors: wouldn't it make sense if there was something in their brains which makes them unable to kill each other? That way the species would have a much better chance of surviving..."

Cruse dismissed Shari's theory as nonsense, and

then remembered something. "Kristas couldn't shoot that StormTrooper who was ready to kill me back on the coast," he reminded her.

"But he had no problem firing at the wolf that attacked me later," Shari realized. "But, Cruse, Kristas couldn't be an Inheritor. The Inheritors evolved into what they are today through dire necessity. Kristas's circumstances have been entirely different. . ."

"Or maybe he's evolving into something else. . ." Barnaby said. "But why is it happening now and so quickly?"

"Can we cut out the hypotheses and the questions?" Cruse said impatiently. "We don't even know if Kristas is still alive! All I want to do is find out what evil and twisted little game Momma Mercy is playing, where the missing Inheritors have gone, and what's happened to the mutants." He turned to Shari. "*And* why you and I are still alive!"

"Alive?"

"If I had been Momma, I would have shot us the first opportunity I had."

"Maybe she thought that the drugged air in the Honeywell would have kept us harmless?" Shari suggested.

"And maybe she's just a sweet old lady who spends all her days studying knitting patterns," Cruse cracked sarcastically. "Now let's go and get some answers!"

210

Beautiful Baby

"This is the place," Shari said to Barnaby, as the three of them walked into the Upper Rooms. It was the first time the young Inheritor had been there, and he looked around nervously, as if expecting guards to leap out of the darkened corners at any minute. He was also reeling from the acute change in atmosphere.

"It's OK," she reassured him. "We're quite safe. Momma thinks her drugs guarantee so much compliance with her wishes that there's no need for any security. You saw how easy it was leaving the Honeywell when we went looking for Cruse."

"The rest of the people here are so numbed and content with their lot, that they don't even think of escaping," Cruse said scornfully. "But Momma's going to start asking questions when she discovers Marla's body."

"This way," said Barnaby, and led them to the door which opened into the honeycombed chamber.

"How do you know where to go?" Shari asked, but it was Cruse who silenced her. They had seen how Kristas had instinctively known where to go; it was hardly surprising that Barnaby, as an Inheritor, would also possess the same ability to some degree.

"It's horrible," decided Barnaby, when he entered the chamber, and looked at the surrounding pods, and the shadowy figures inside them swimming in the life-giving nutrients. "Perverting the course of nature like this. Creating people out of test-tubes."

Cruse agreed with him with feeling; he was still hurting over Maria. "The Honeywell covers most of the southern half of this country," he said. "Momma needs as many Helpers as she can get: this is as good a way as any to get them. And all of them subservient to her commands; you don't get any free will with clones, unlike humans who have this annoying tendency occasionally to think for themselves."

"But on this scale?" Shari marvelled. There had to be at least a hundred pods in the chamber, all of them harbouring clones in varying degrees of development. "She must be a genius."

"She certainly is," agreed Cruse. "But what I want to know is why she's remained hidden from the System for so long."

"She knew the System from within," Shari reminded him. "She knows its methods. And she told us herself that she'd faked her own death, and that the System had long forgotten about this place."

"You still shouldn't be able to stay undiscovered by the Child Roland for long," Cruse said. "He's a sneaky scuzzball; his spies are everywhere."

Shari nodded, even though she remembered being quite taken by news shots of Roland, when she and Cruse had hacked into System news transmission; he looked so cute and innocent, the sort of person you could rely on, and the kind of man who wouldn't hurt a fly. That was the secret of his success, Cruse had once told her; when someone looks as if they wouldn't hurt a fly then that was the time for all those flies to watch out.

"What has she done to the Inheritors?" Shari asked. "And the mutants?"

"They're behind here," Barnaby said, and walked up the steps to the large double doors, from behind which Shari had heard that strange sound which reminded her of a giant heartbeat.

"How do you know – " she started to ask, and then smiled. "OK – you just know, that's all!"

Cruse followed them up to the door, and ran his hand over the surface. "Clever," he said appreciatively to himself. "Trisilicate."

"What's that?" asked Barnaby.

"It's a special kind of alloy," he explained. "But it's

not manufactured like your normal alloys – it's grown like a crystal –"

"I thought it felt organic. . ."

Cruse passed his hand over the opening mechanism which failed to activate. He grinned at Shari. "It seems that Momma isn't quite that trusting!" he said, and fired at the device with his zip-gun.

"Is that how you solve every problem, Cruse?" Barnaby asked, and then fell silent as the door slid open, and they walked into the room beyond.

Drum. Drum. Drum.

The sound of a giant heartbeat filled the entire room, pounding deep into Shari, Cruse and Barnaby's very bodies, churning their stomachs so much that each of them feared they were going to throw up. Struggling to keep the bile from rising in their throats they looked around the room.

The walls were greyly functional, covered with all manner of equipment, the purpose of which they knew they would never be able to understand. Fifteen chairs lined one wall, and strapped into every one of them were the missing Inheritors. Each of them was wearing a helmet, or skullcap, similar to the one Shari had seen Casterbridge wearing in the "hospital ward". Each helmet was attached to a large overhead monitor, displaying their brain patterns.

The Inheritors stared unblinkingly ahead, more dead than alive. Casterbridge, who had been the oldest of them, now seemed little more than a barely living skeleton, his thin skin translucent, and pulled tightly over his cheekbones. Shari rushed up to him, and attempted to unstrap him from his chair, but was prevented from doing so by Cruse.

"Leave him be for the moment," he advised. "At least he's still alive. Unhooking him from that thing might kill him."

"Alice!" Barnaby ran to the chair nearest a large archway which led into another room. It was from this room that the "heartbeat" was coming.

Alice was attached to a "helmet" like all the others, but there was still some life in her eyes, probably because she had been under the influence of the machine for such a short time. She gazed at Barnaby, Shari and Cruse, and they saw the look of recognition in her eyes.

"Alice, what are you doing here?" Barnaby asked. Alice didn't answer, but instead moved her eyes, indicating the room beyond the archway.

"Kristas. . ." she finally managed to say, and Shari, Cruse and Barnaby raced through the archway. Only Cruse had the good sense to take his zip-gun out of its holster.

The room beyond, bigger even than the honeycombed chamber, was a laboratory, but the sort of laboratory they could never have conjured up in all their wildest imaginings.

Computers and giant smart-boxes covered every available piece of wall-space, whirring and chattering to each other like a billion bees in a hive. Along the ceiling, huge transparent tubes hung, filled with a blue-green liquid, which reminded Shari of the nutrients being pumped into the clones' pods in the honeycombed chamber.

A vast video screen took up one entire wall, upon which complicated chemical equations and elaborate three-dimensional charts were displayed in dizzying succession. Shari recognised, amongst them, a graphic representation of the DNA molecule.

On long wooden workbenches (mahogany, Cruse noticed with interest) the contents of a thousand testtubes bubbled, and in transparent cages, munching away at their food, were small animals: chimps with three eyes instead of two, gnome-like creatures covered with bristles and quills, their wide eyes full of fear, and – this was worst of all – a creature that had the body of a lupe, but the face of a man. And in a hundred specimen jars and Petri dishes, a hundred smaller monsters crept and crawled. Shari remembered the mutant beast she had found in the circle of stones: it had obviously escaped from the Honeywell, from the place where it had been created.

In the centre of the laboratory, dominating the entire chamber was a huge transparent cylinder, into which the overhead tubes snaked, pumping in the viscous blue-green liquid.

And swimming about in the life-giving nutrients in the cylinder, was a creature, a monster so horrible, and so noisome that Shari found it difficult not to retch.

It was about five feet tall, and its huge, bulbous head was attached to several copper electrodes, which in turn were connected to a generator suspended from the ceiling above the open top of the cylinder, and from which a vile stench emanated.

The creature's head was transparent, and Shari could see its brain as it pumped and pulsated. Unlike a human brain, which is composed of only two cerebrum hemispheres, this creature's brain seemed to be made of up three separate, yet interconnected, lumps of matter.

The creature's eyes, bloodshot and out of proportion even to its giant head, darted uncomprehendingly this way and that, trying to make sense of its surroundings, and its mouth opened and closed, gulping in the life-giving nutrients which surrounded it. Its face was covered with pustules and sores, from which pus and blood oozed freely.

Huge muscular arms flailed about in the surrounding liquid, bashing themselves against the walls of its transparent prison, as if trying to escape. Its stubby fingers ended in razor sharp nails, and Shari cringed as she heard them scraping and squeaking down the sides of its transparent prison. Strange tubular organs tumbled out of its body, floating and waving in the thick liquid, as the creature writhed and twisted in its own blood and vomit.

To Shari, it brought to mind nothing less than a monstrous human embryo, perverted beyond all recognition. She looked over at Cruse, and Barnaby, both of whom were as white as sheets. In an instinctive reflex action, Cruse raised his zip-gun and prepared to fire at the Creature. Barnaby shook his head, and pulled down Cruse's arm.

"What is it?" Shari asked. Her throat was dry and her voice was cracked.

"Isn't he beautiful?"

Everyone turned in the direction of the voice. Momma Mercy was entering the chamber through a door at the far end of the room. Cruse growled with hatred, but didn't shoot. Momma, for her part, didn't seem in the slightest bit concerned that a gun had just been trained on her.

"What is it?" Cruse demanded, hoping that his voice didn't betray the sickness he felt in the presence of the creature.

"It's Momma's new baby," the old woman cooed. "Isn't he gorgeous?"

"He's an ugly brute," Cruse spat out the words, keeping his eye on both the monster in the glass cage and Momma Mercy.

Momma affected a look of disappointment. "He's what you might become one day, my poppet," she said, and smiled when she saw the looks of incomprehension on the faces of Shari, Cruse and Barnaby.

"What do you mean?" Shari asked, and stared at

the creature; it stared back at her, sending shivers down her spine.

"The ultimate stage in the course of human evolution," she announced rather grandly. "It's been my project for ten years now – the creation and breeding from basic genetic material of *homo superior*!"

"That *thing* is what we'll evolve into?" Barnaby asked.

"With a little friendly persuasion and genetic engineering from its loving Momma, of course," Momma replied pleasantly. She glanced over quickly at Cruse; he had lowered his zip-gun.

"It's evil," Shari said. "It's horrible..."

"Imperfect, perhaps," Momma said sadly. "It has the strength of twenty men, has marvellous recuperative powers, and can survive anywhere, from the coldest depths of the ocean to the scorching deserts of TerraNova..."

TerraNova, Cruse noticed but kept his thoughts to himself. *She didn't call it Mars...*

"But there is one thing it's lacking," Momma said. "One talent absent in *homo sapiens*, which it needs if it truly is to become the beauty of the world..."

"That's why you need the Inheritors," Barnaby suddenly realized. "That's why you're monitoring their brain patterns back there in the other room! You want their psychic abilities!"

Momma laughed. "Your telepathic talents are hardly developed," she said. "My machines are showing me that. I've already created clones with more psychic potential than you..."

"Muhajji," Shari suddenly realized, and remembered reading his case notes in Momma's Baby Book. *Psi potential: Thirty-three.*

"That's right," Momma said. "I knew that a group of Inheritors were living somewhere near London, but I had no idea where. That's why I sent Muhajji there – to use his own psi-abilities to track them down. But even he had no idea of what he would find. He sensed the presence of one person – and not an Inheritor, my child! – who had it in him to be one of the greatest psychics in the System. A genetic aberration, a hiccup on the part of Nature, someone whose telepathic powers have developed way beyond what they should have done for this point in human evolution."

"But who?" asked Shari, although she was already sure she knew the answer.

She followed Momma's gaze to a darkened corner of the room, which had been set up like an operating theatre. There, strapped to a bed, just as the mutants and Inheritors had been in the hospital ward, was the person she had lost all hope of ever seeing again.

"Kristas!" she cried, and ran over to his bedside. Momma made no attempt to stop her, but sauntered casually after her.

Kristas was connected to a series of drips and wires, which were suspended over his bed. He looked at Shari with glazed and drugged eyes, which hardly recognized her.

"I wouldn't disturb him, if I were you," Momma said.

"What have you done with him?" Shari demanded. "What are you going to do with him?"

"Operate on him," Momma said, as casually as if she were discussing a shopping list. "Identify that part of his brain which has outpaced natural evolution and isolate it."

"'Outpaced natural evolution'?" Shari asked. "I don't understand..."

"All humans have in them great psychic potential," Momma Mercy explained airily. "In many tens of thousands of years, evolution shall take its course and we will all be as telepathic as our young friend here."

Shari looked back at the monster writhing in its tank. "But what has that got to do with that monster...?"

Momma Mercy winced at Shari's description. "Momma's baby is mildly telepathic," she said. "Oh, Momma is very clever, you see. A judicious crossing-over of certain synapses in the brain, a skilful mutation of certain dendrites, and her babies are granted some psychic ability." She sighed. "But the process isn't complete, for, alas, I am not God."

"That hasn't stopped you from *playing* at God,"

Cruse remarked, and Momma cast him an evil look before continuing.

"The Other has reached out its mind, and contacted Kristas Chernenko, linking its thoughts to his," Momma said. "Perhaps that's what sparked off your friend's psychic abilities, nurturing and bringing to life what had long remained dormant in his brain. When I identify that ability I can transfer it to the Other –" she glanced briefly at the monster in its cage – "and endow it with the same telepathic abilities as our young friend here. My baby's psi-powers are artificially created, and – much as it pains his Momma to say so – hopelessly inadequate for the task I have prepared for him. But when I match Chernenko's natural abilities to my own baby's –"

"Like hell you will," Cruse said, and raised his zip-gun once more and pointed it at Momma Mercy. "Now, release Kristas."

Momma smiled evilly, and a shaft of super-concentrated light shot across the chamber, knocking Cruse's gun out of his hand. Shari reached for her own zip-gun, and that too was shot from her.

They both turned to see who had fired the shots, and a familiar figure stepped out of the shadows, followed by several of Momma's cloned Helpers, who roughly grabbed Shari, Cruse and Barnaby in grips of steel. The Helpers were too strong even for Cruse to resist; Momma had made sure of that when she had bred them.

"Trueheart!" Cruse spat out the name, as he recognized the leader of the System. Donovan Trueheart nodded him a sarcastic welcome, and replaced his plasma-gun in the folds of his scarlet tunic. He walked up to Cruse, and Cruse turned his face away when he smelt the sour stink of alcohol on the Trueheart's breath.

"We meet again, mercenary," the Trueheart said. "You and your friends have caused me a lot of trouble since you escaped from the System three years ago. You have become an example to all the malcontents who do not realize just how much the Trueheart loves them..."

"So kill us," Cruse said defiantly, but the Trueheart shook his head.

"And lose a valuable propaganda tool?" he laughed. "Your exploits have inspired a whole generation of young ne'er-do-wells who are rebelling against the System. You must be brought back to TerraNova and made an example of..."

"So that's why we've been allowed to go on living," Cruse realized. "You want to put on a show trial, before executing us..."

"It will be on all the prime-time networks, if that's any consolation," the Trueheart said. "But there is another reason." He looked over at Momma Mercy, who had come over to join him. Cruse, Shari and Barnaby stared hatefully at the old woman who had said she had been working against the System for the past ten years, when all the time she had been in Donovan Trueheart's secret employ.

"For me to successfully identify and extract the part of Kristas Chernenko's brain which supports his telepathic abilities, he must submit willingly to my laser-scalpel," she said. "If he closes off that part of his mind, then there will be no point in the operation."

"Kristas would never agree to something like that," Shari protested. "He'd never help the System!"

"Aha, my dear," said the Trueheart, "But he would if he knew that his two closest friends were being held hostage... You see, you're *much* more useful to Momma and myself alive..."

Shari glared hatefully at her tormentor, and at Momma Mercy. "Why did you tell us you were working against the System?" she asked her.

"It suited my purposes," Momma replied. "Besides, I doubt if the mutants who have sought sanctuary over the years would have come here if they had known the truth."

"The mutants who live here," Shari said. "Why do they keep disappearing? Where have they gone?"

Momma smiled, and looked over at the Other, swimming and twisting in its life-giving waters.

"Broken down, pulped and pulverized, the Mutes make a very tasty soup for my baby," she said. "Mutes are very full of rich nutrients you know..." She frowned when she saw the look of distaste on

Shari's face. "Don't look so disgusted, my poppet. After all, have you gone without a hungry belly since you arrived at Honeywell?"

Momma Mercy clucked impatiently, like a mother hen. "Now, can we get working?" she asked irritably. "My beautiful big baby is anxious to be born..."

Identity Crisis

"So what's in it for you, Trueheart?" Cruse demanded hours later. He, Shari and Barnaby had been placed under the armed guard of Momma's clones, and sequestered in a small room, adjacent to the chamber containing the Other, where Momma Mercy was performing the operation on Kristas.

"The joy of knowing that I have brought another life into the world," the Trueheart claimed loftily.

"Don't give us that," Shari snapped. "Your plans are much more basic."

The Trueheart considered the three young people before him. It wasn't wise to tell them his plans, but the Trueheart had already drunk another bottle of Olympus Mons, and besides, there was no one else to whom he could brag.

"When the Other is finally whole, he will be totally respondent to my will," he claimed. "I shall use him – and the Others like him that Momma will breed for me – to restore order in the System..."

"Restore order?" Cruse repeated, and then laughed. "The System's finally turned against you, Trueheart! That's why you're down here on Earth, throwing in your lot with the Mutes and the misfits like us!"

Donovan Trueheart's face fell. "There is merely a minor local difficulty," he lied. "It shall be over in a matter of days."

In truth, there had been more than a "little local difficulty". Somehow the flight recorder from Schreck's battlecruiser had been discovered by a band of youngsters not entirely happy with Donovan Trueheart's presidency of the System. The Trueheart had no idea how they had gained possession of the recorder, and the Child Roland claimed that he didn't know either.

Roland had tried to contain the damage (*System bless him!* thought the Trueheart gratefully), but its discovery proved to have a snowball effect. Questions were asked about the Trueheart's extravagant lifestyle on the Island, and people who were starving envied him his ever-widening girth. The Child Roland, as slim as ever, had reassured the people that His Magnificence had become fat not through over-eating, but because of an unusual thyroid problem (he had even produced the forged medical records to substantiate the claim).

For a while, the people believed the lie, until a band of rebels discovered the Trueheart's personal vineyards down on TerraNova, and were shocked at the abundance of food and drink which the Trueheart had had stored there.

It was then that the Child Roland had faced the Trueheart's wrath, with the System President demanding why the vineyards hadn't been guarded by security troops as was customary. But then his anger with his trusted aide-de-camp softened when Roland explained that he had had the guards transferred to a connurbation on the other side of the planet, to back up their colleagues who were dealing with a full-scale riot.

(The Trueheart had asked to see holo-images of the rioting, but the Child Roland had advised against it. Allegedly, the scenes were too violent and bloody for the Trueheart's great sensitivity.)

The Trueheart was delighted that someone like Roland still cared so much for him, and had followed the Child's advice when he had suggested that he fly to the Home Planet for a few days to check up on Momma's progress, and stay away from "all this unpleasantness", as he had termed it.

"What's it like not to be loved, Trueheart?" Cruse taunted him.

228

"The people love me with all their heart," the Trueheart claimed, uncertainly.

"After you've starved them for years?" Shari asked. "After you've cold-bloodedly destroyed an entire planet of innocent souls?"

The Trueheart turned angrily on Shari, and, taking advantage of his diverted attention, and keeping one eye on the security guard at the door, Barnaby passed the zip-gun he had to Cruse. Barnaby wasn't able to operate the thing, but he knew that Cruse would put it to good use.

"What does it matter?" The Trueheart said. "With the Other they will know to fear me. Indeed, if Momma's work is successful they will never question my will again."

"What do you mean?" asked Barnaby.

"The ultimate creature possessed of the greatest psychic powers this System has ever known, courtesy of your friend Kristas," the Trueheart said, a maniacal glint in his eye. "Why, its mental powers might be so great that it could bend the entire System to my will!"

"Creating a bunch of ineffectual mindless zombies, I suppose," Cruse said with disgust.

"A united people in a System happily living under the Trueheart," Donovan Trueheart corrected him.

The Trueheart turned around, as he heard Momma call him from the laboratory. He bade the three of them farewell, and then changed his mind. He ordered the guard to escort them into the laboratory;

he wanted them to witness his and Momma's triumph.

Shari's first concern was for Kristas. She looked over to the bed where Momma had operated on him. He was still connected to the overhead drips, and a monitor at the side of his bed emitted a regular series of blips, indicating that his heart was still beating. His head was covered with cotton gauze, which at least proved that Momma still wanted him alive, even after she had operated on him.

Then she turned to the Other, the creature that had been calling across the distances to Kristas, drawing him to the Honeywell as surely as a magnet to iron. It seemed more vibrant somehow, as if whatever Momma had taken from Kristas's brain and implanted into its cerebellum had imbued it with a new and unnatural strength.

It twisted in its soup of nutrients, staring at each of them – the Trueheart, Momma Mercy, Shari, Cruse and Barnaby – in turn, before resting its gaze on Kristas, still unconscious on the bed, and surrounded by several of Momma's Little Helpers, clad in their customary green tunics. A strange sound came from its slit of a mouth, as it regarded Kristas; it was a mournful, almost angry sound.

"Momma, I congratulate you," said the Trueheart, and planted a kiss on the old woman's wizened cheek. She was beaming with pride, as if she were a young woman again who had just given birth to her very own child, rather than the cold and scheming genetic manipulator she really was.

The Trueheart turned back to Shari and the others, a triumphant smile on his face. "Rebels, I give you *homo superior*!" he exclaimed. "The first in a new species that will ensure that our glorious System will go on for yet another thousand years!"

"Really?" said Cruse, and whipped out of his pocket the zip-gun which Barnaby had passed to him. Before any of Momma's armed Helpers could react, he aimed it directly at the glass tank and fired.

The cylinder exploded into a thousand splinters, and the thick blue-green ooze which had filled it gushed out, flooding the laboratory floor, and filling the entire room with its stomach-churning stink of death.

The Other screeched out in terror, as it was finally released from its prison. It leapt out, and swayed uncertainly for a few moments as it regained its sense of balance, and its specially designed lungs readjusted themselves to its new environment of oxygen-rich atmosphere. Shards of glass had become embedded in its skin, and trickles of crimson blood poured out of scores of tiny wounds.

Then something inside it suddenly seemed to snap. Shari watched on in horror, as its brain, visible beneath its transparent skull, pumped and pumped, until it seemed that it would explode. The Other lashed out with mighty, muscled arms, upturning a whole workbench laden with jars of chemicals, which smashed, releasing their noxious and deadly fumes into the honeyed atmosphere.

"Momma! Do something!" Trueheart cried, but Momma Mercy had already taken to her heels and was racing out of the lab, followed by her Helpers.

The Trueheart took out his gun and fired at the creature, but it seemed to have no effect on its enormous bulk. It swiped out at Trueheart, knocking him to the floor, before turning its attention to a bank of computers lining the wall. It started to pound savagely on them, and they exploded in a shower of sparks. A massive dose of electricity surged through its body, and, for one horrible second, its skin became totally translucent, and Shari could clearly see the bones beneath it.

"Let's get out of here!" Cruse said, as the monster continued on its rampage of destruction, apparently unharmed by the massive electrical shock which, if anything, had seemed only further to enrage it.

"Not without Kristas!" shouted Shari, struggling to make herself heard above the sound of smashing glass and exploding equipment.

"You're crazy!" Cruse protested, although he too joined Shari and Barnaby as they unhooked Kristas from his drips, and released him from the leather straps which had bound his body to the bed. His eyes fluttered open, and he seemed to recognize them, as he allowed himself to be helped out of the lab.

Of Momma Mercy and Donovan Trueheart, there was no sign. And as Shari, Cruse, Kristas and Barnaby headed for the elevators which would take them to the surface they could still hear the cries of agony and anger of the Other as it struck helplessly at its new home, tormented and confused, and wanting only escape and sanctuary from its unbearable pain.

"We can't leave the others, we *must* go back!" Shari said resolutely, once they had reached the relative safety of their skimmer on the surface. By her side, Kristas had regained full consciousness. Although he still wore the strip of white cloth around his head, he was now feeling perfectly fine; in the thirty-third century recovery from surgery was always quick and efficient.

"We do that and we're dead meat," Cruse said. "That thing's insane. Donovan Trueheart wanted a killing machine: it looks like Momma's been a little too successful."

"No, it's hurt, confused."

Everyone turned to look at Kristas.

"It's been imprisoned for ten years, while Momma experimented on it, tortured it. Now all it wants is an end to all its suffering..."

"How do you know?" Shari asked.

"I know," was the inevitable answer.

"I thought Momma had taken away that part of

your brain dedicated to your psi-abilities?" Barnaby said, but Kristas just shrugged.

"It seems she doesn't quite understand fully what she's been doing," he said.

"We have to go back to the Honeywell, Cruse," Shari insisted. "The rest of the Inheritors are still there – we must save them. And so are the mutants –"

"The ones that haven't been killed in Momma's experiments," Cruse reminded here.

"Please, Cruse," Shari begged.

"And just how do you think we're going to defend ourselves against that thing with just one measly zip-gun?" Cruse asked. He thought for a moment, stroking his chin. "What we need is some weapon, powerful enough to blast that monster away once and for all – and Trueheart too, if we're lucky." He looked slyly at Barnaby. "The Inheritance?"

"No, Cruse," Barnaby said. "The Inheritance is only to be used in the direst emergency."

"And I suppose this doesn't qualify?" Cruse asked sarcastically. "Fifteen of your people – probably the last hope for the human race – trapped down in the Honeywell with a creature from hell that'll probably rip them apart limb by limb, before setting its sights on the rest of the System? And possibly a chance to wipe out Trueheart and Momma Mercy at the same time?"

It was a persuasive argument, and Barnaby was forced to concede. The four of them went to the

234

clump of berry bushes where they had hidden the Inheritance. Carefully regulating the power on his zip-gun, Cruse fired a beam of energy at the wooden box, neatly blasting its lid off.

"Now, we'll see some action," said Cruse, and licked his lips with anticipation as he went over to the opened box. He peered over the edge to examine its contents, and his face fell.

"Books?" he said in disbelief.

The others joined him, and Shari took out some of the old-fashioned leather-bound volumes which had been stored in the airtight box for hundreds of years. She read out a few of their titles: *The Mayor of Casterbridge*; *The Origin of Species*; *Alice in Wonderland*; *The Wind in the Willows*.

"I don't understand," she said. "This is your Inheritance, Barnaby?"

Barnaby – who had been shocked to find his name on the cover of one of the books (*Barnaby Rudge*, which apparently had been written by someone called Charles Dickens) – shook his head.

"I don't know," he finally admitted. "None of us knew what the Inheritance really was; all we knew was that it was supposed to be a source of great power...

Cruse laughed. "It looks as though we've well and truly been made idiots of. That settles it, we're not going back to the Honeywell."

"We have to, Cruse!" Shari insisted again. "We

have to save the Inheritors and the mutants from that creature..."

Cruse was having none of it, and he picked up one of the books: *Crop Cultivation and Animal Husbandry*.

"And what do you suggest we do, Shari?" he asked sarcastically. "Hit it where it hurts with one of these?"

"No," said Kristas. "For once we're not going to resort to violence."

"Dream on, Dreamer," Cruse said.

"We are going to go back to the Honeywell, but not with guns and weapons," Kristas said. "For once, we're going to use this."

And with a grin, Kristas tapped at his temple with his forefinger.

The upper levels of the Honeywell were in ruins. The laboratory in which the Other had been birthed was now a smoking mess of chemicals and wrecked electrical equipment, which the Other had destroyed in its rage. Here and there small electrical fires sparked, and flamed, although greater damage had been prevented by Momma's automatic sprinkler system, which was raining down flame-quenching water.

Shari raised her lips to the rush of water: it tasted good and pure, she thought, and presumed that it came from the underground streams which snaked their way through the lower reaches of the Honey-

236

well. If they ever got out of here alive, that could be an important new source of fresh water for them, she realized.

They passed through the honeycombed chamber – all of the pods had been smashed open, and their occupants had been either dragged out or had fallen out. Shari and Barnaby turned away in horror at the sickening sight of half-formed clones, flapping about helplessly on the floor like fishes out of water.

Others, more developed, crawled about on all-fours, scarcely knowing where they were, and too weak to stand up. Cruse, filled with hatred for the perverted products of Momma's experiments, kicked one. Kristas turned on him.

"What the System did you do that for?" he cried.

"They're freaks, no better than Trueheart and the others," Cruse replied, although even he thought that he might have gone a little too far this time. He would never admit it to Kristas, of course.

"They're living creatures!" Kristas said angrily. "No matter how they've been created, they're not evil themselves!"

"They're clones, little better than zombies or ServoRobots," Cruse said. "The System can bend them to its will."

"And maybe away from the System they can think for themselves," Kristas argued. "Maybe there they can find their freedom." And he turned away from Cruse, and murmured, half to himself, "Besides, I haven't come here to hurt anyone, I'm here to save lives – and one life in particular..."

"What did you say?" Cruse demanded, but Kristas refused to answer. Instead, and, much to Shari and Cruse's surprise, he started to take charge.

"Barnaby, you attend to the remaining Inheritors in the antechamber to the lab," he ordered. "Remove their helmets and unstrap them and get them out of here."

"Isn't that dangerous?" Shari asked. "Removing those helmets might kill them."

"They're only monitoring their brain patterns," Kristas told her, and Barnaby left them to do as instructed. "Remember I was in Momma's lab – I know."

"As you're so busy giving orders, what do you suggest we do?" Cruse asked.

"We find as many mutants as we can and lead them up to the surface," Kristas said. "And then we find the Other..."

Cruse smiled evilly and fingered the zip-gun at his side. "And how do you propose we do that?" he asked, and walked out on to the gantry which overlooked the Honeywell. "There are about forty levels down there. How do we know where it is?"

"He's calling out to me," Kristas said, "in my mind. I'll know where to find him."

"*It*," Cruse corrected him. "Not him."

"*Him*," Kristas insisted, and Cruse eyed him suspiciously. He looked around for Shari; she had followed Barnaby into the antechamber to the lab and was helping him free the dazed Inheritors. Just to the side of the row of chairs, there was a large bank of instruments, and Cruse went up to examine it. It emitted a steady humming sound, and from one of the many grilles on it came a rasping noise, almost like someone breathing.

"What is it?" Shari asked, at the same time carefully freeing Alice from her bonds.

Cruse grinned. "A breath of fresh air," he chuckled, and indicated the dials and levers. "It looks like it controls the flow of air around the Honeywell."

"Momma's air-conditioning unit!" Shari realized. "The thing that's keeping everyone docile and subservient to her."

"That's right," Cruse said, and added wryly, "Pity it doesn't do the same thing for our monster friend as well." He reached out and rammed down a lever, closing the system down. The machine fell silent. "That'll wake up a few people in this place," he decided, and together with Shari he followed Kristas out of the lab, and down into the Honeywell.

Within ten minutes, chaos reigned in the Honeywell, as Cruse's handiwork had its effect. With Momma's drugged air no longer circulating, the surviving mutants started to remember the things they had been conditioned to forget.

They recalled the screams of some of their fellows, as they had been dragged off by Momma's Helpers, their bodies destined to be broken down and used as nutrients for the birthing of the Other. And then they remembered the wonderful foods that had often been placed at their tables in the Honeywell's communal dining areas, and wondered whether they had been eating their own kind.

For some, the shock of realization was too much to bear, and their minds snapped, and they ran screaming and senseless through the corridors of the Honeywell, or lay curled up in a darkened corner, whimpering to themselves.

Others simply wanted to escape and as Shari, Cruse and Kristas descended into the lowest levels of the Honeywell, they encountered mutants running, as if for their lives, up to the surface, to a world poisoned and barren but which now seemed much more welcoming than the luxurious greenness of Momma's Honeywell.

And others were consumed with a blind and all-encompassing hate for Donovan Trueheart and Momma Mercy. Arming themselves with whatever weapons they could find – the branches of trees, knives, even the laser-rifles of a group of four of Momma's Helpers whom they had waylaid and attacked – they went off in search of their erstwhile tormentors.

With the sound of the rampaging mutants ringing

in their ears, Shari and her friends reached the floor of the Honeywell. Kristas raced out of the elevator, and ran into the wooded glade, with Shari and Cruse following him.

Even without Kristas to guide them it would have been an easy matter to find the Other. Small trees had been uprooted where it had passed, leaving a trail of devastation that was simple to follow. They found the Other on the shores of a small lake, staring at its own reflection, and growling softly to itself.

It registered their presence, and turned round, snarling. It pulled itself back on its haunches, ready to pounce. Cruse raised his zip-gun to shoot at the creature, but Kristas knocked the gun savagely out of his hand with such force that it flew away and into the lake.

"What the System did you do that for?" Cruse demanded angrily, for a second ignoring the savage beast only a few metres away from them.

"There will be no more killing!" Kristas told him, in a tone of voice neither Cruse nor Shari had ever heard him use before.

"Thank you, Kristas," came a despised voice from their left.

They all turned around – even the Other, who growled, angry like a baited bear – to see Donovan Trueheart smiling at them. He was accompanied by Momma Mercy, and, unlike Cruse, he had a gun.

"I was right!" Cruse said angrily to Shari. "Kristas has been working for Trueheart all along!"

The Trueheart shook his head. "He has served our purposes, provided us with his psi-abilities to transfer into that creature," he said. "But he has never been in our employ."

The Other stalked towards the now defenceless Cruse, Kristas and Shari, huge globs of acidic saliva dripping from its ugly mouth. As it prepared to spring, Kristas dashed forwards, never once taking his eyes from those of the creature for a second.

The creature roared angrily, and for a moment Shari thought that it was going to lash out at Kristas. And then it quietened down and regarded Kristas curiously.

"What's he doing?" Shari asked, and even the Trueheart and Momma Mercy looked on, confused yet fascinated.

"Blast it, he's communicating with the ugly brute!" Cruse suddenly realized, and remembered Kristas telling him that it was time to use their minds. "He's talking telepathically to it!"

You don't have to be frightened of me, Kristas thought, the large vein at his temple throbbing, and sheets of sweat pouring down his brow. *We mean you no harm.*

The Other started to whimper. *Cold, so cold*, it seemed to be saying. *It was so warm in the blue-green waters... But they hurt me even there... Ten long years... So alone... And yet never alone...*

How can we help? Kristas asked.

There is no help. No escape...

Escape?

Release from the thousands upon thousands of souls inside me. Crying out inside my head, tearing my senses apart.

With a shock, Kristas suddenly realized what the Other was referring to. Artificially created from millions of separate cells, and feeding off the nutrients distilled from thousands of mutants, the Other had somehow inherited all their memories.

It was something not even Momma Mercy could have foreseen: the Other, *homo superior*, the supposed future of the human race was having a mammoth identity crisis!

Come with us, Kristas urged. *We can help you...*

No help for me ... no future ... no sanctuary...

Donovan Trueheart walked forwards, no longer fearing the Other now that Kristas – he wasn't quite sure how – had rendered the creature docile. The Other saw the flash of crimson of the Trueheart's cloak, and turned. He growled, instinctively recognizing in the Trueheart the man who was ultimately responsible for his birth and for his unending torment. With an angry roar, he leapt on to Donovan Trueheart.

The Trueheart was too quick for him. He whipped

out his gun from his cloak and shot the creature full in the stomach, which exploded in a mess of flesh and blood. The Other staggered back, but amazingly did not fall, and turned on the Trueheart again.

Panicking, the Trueheart unleashed the full charge of his blaster on him. With a screech of such agony that it would haunt the dreams of Shari, Cruse and Kristas for the rest of their lives, the Other crashed to the floor, dead, a steaming, bloody carcass.

From somewhere out of the undergrowth rushed Gabriel, and started to feast on the fresh meat.

"You killed him," Momma Mercy said, and sniffed tearfully. "You killed my baby..."

"He didn't want to harm anyone." Kristas said. "He didn't even want to be born..."

Still shaken by the attack on him, the Trueheart didn't notice Cruse until it was too late. The young mercenary ran towards him, head-butting him in the belly, and knocking the System President to the ground. The Trueheart's gun fell out of his hand.

Three years ago Donovan Trueheart and Cruse had been face-to-face and Cruse had always regretted not using that opportunity to do what he had always wanted to. Now he wasn't going to let the chance pass again: he was going to kill Donovan Trueheart. He reached up for the older man's throat and squeezed.

A little way off from him, Gabriel looked up, licked his blood-stained lips, and considered the two men rolling around on the ground. Lupes were widely regarded as one of the most loyal and savage animals in the System, and it was said that they would defend their masters to the very death. The lion/wolf cross-breed twitched its snout for a moment and then returned to its feast: in the System there were more important things than loyalty. Things like food, for instance.

Despite his bulk, and the damage inflicted on his body by too much meat and drink, the Trueheart was far stronger than he appeared. With a mighty heave he managed to wrest Cruse's hands off his body, and push the younger man away. Staggering to his feet, he reached out for his gun, and cried out in pain when Shari's foot came down on his wrist. There was a horrible snapping sound, as his wristbone broke. Kristas reached down and swiped the gun from his grasp, and pointed it at the Trueheart.

"Fire it!" ordered Cruse, who was getting to his feet. "Kill the scum!"

Kristas's hand shook. "I can't!" he cried. "It's impossible for me! I can't kill!"

Taking advantage of the momentary delay, the Trueheart ran forwards and snatched the gun from Kristas's hand. He swung it in a wide arc, covering Cruse, Kristas and Shari. Defenceless, they huddled together, steeling themselves for the blast they knew from the Trueheart's sadistic stare would surely come. In the confusion, Momma Mercy had vanished.

The Trueheart was standing in front of a clump of bushes, and suddenly a hand – scabbed and oozing with sores – reached out through the foliage, and wrapped itself around the Trueheart's neck. Once again, the Trueheart's gun fell to the ground, and Cruse wasted no time in diving down and seizing it.

Donovan Trueheart looked in horror, as he felt the sharp edge of a knife graze his skin, and he gazed up at the sneering and scarred face of one of the mutants his System had used and abused for so long.

Shari recognized him as Ganymede, the mutant they had first met in the circle of stones, and who she had believed had been killed by Momma to feed the Other. Now, released from Momma's conditioning, he and his fellows had reached the bottom of the Honeywell, and were out for vengeance.

Yet Ganymede and the other mutants were still weak, and, like Cruse, Ganymede underestimated the Trueheart's strength. The System President elbowed the mutant in the stomach, and freeing himself from his grip, raced into the undergrowth. Cruse fired, and started to make chase, when the sound of someone yelling stopped him.

He turned to see Barnaby running towards them. In a second he took in the dead body of the Other (still being gnawed upon by the hungry Gabriel), and then turned to Cruse.

"We have to get out now!" he cried.

"First we get Trueheart," Cruse said. Ganymede and a band of about ten mutants who had joined him muttered their agreement.

"You don't understand," Barnaby said. "Can't you feel that rumbling beneath your feet?"

Sure enough, the ground was trembling.

"It's Momma," he said. "She's set the Honeywell's self-destruct system into operation. She knows she's defeated – and she's going to make sure that everything and everyone goes with her!"

"But how?" Shari said. "She was here only a few moments ago."

"She activated it when the Other went berserk," Barnaby said. "The clones told me –'

"The clones? Momma's Little Helpers?"

"With Momma out of the way they're starting to think for themselves," Barnaby said. "They want to help us."

Kristas shot Cruse a look. *See, I was right about that too*, it seemed to say. *Perhaps you should start trusting people more, Cruse!*

"So what were Momma and Trueheart doing down here if the whole thing's about to blow?" Cruse asked, still not certain whether he believed Barnaby or not.

"There are service tunnels under here," Ganymede said. "They lead to the surface. . ."

"Cruse! For once in your life, will you listen to

others!" Shari raged. "We'll all be killed while you stand around here dithering!"

Shari grabbed Cruse's hand and followed Kristas and Barnaby back to the lift. She stopped and turned to Ganymede and his band of mutants. "You're not coming with us?"

Ganymede shook his head. "By experimenting on us and treating us as little more than human cattle, the Trueheart and his kind have made our lives nothing more than a living hell," he said icily. "Now it is time that we had our revenge..."

The Magnificent Donovan Trueheart paused for breath and leant against a wall, looking nervously about in the shadows. The tunnel seemed to be empty, and once again he congratulated himself on his forethought. When he and Momma had rebuilt and fitted out the Honeywell secretly ten years ago, in their great quest to create new life, he had always envisaged that one day things might go wrong, and that the mutants might rebel, or the army of drones and killing machines bred in Momma's tanks might start thinking for themselves. That was why he had had these tunnels built, as an escape route to the surface.

Donovan Trueheart took his smart-box out of his robes, and tapped in a highest-security number, which would connect him almost instantly with the Island in space. He didn't dare try and leave the Earth in his own skimmer – Cruse and his blasted cronies would probably commandeer it anyway – so he would have to call in the help once more of the Child Roland.

While he waited for his connection to be made, he smiled at the thought of the Child Roland. It had been Momma who had introduced the young man to him, and Roland had proved himself to be his most loyal servant through the years, efficient, hard-working and an undisputed master of manipulation. In his own way, the Trueheart loved Roland as the son he never had. He recalled that Momma had once told him that Roland's parents were dead – he certainly never talked about them; perhaps the Trueheart could adopt him as his own.

Finally the connection between Donovan Trueheart's smart-box and the Island were made. The handsome, smiling face of the Child Roland appeared on the smart-box's tiny screen.

"Your Magnificence," Roland said, and chuckled.

"Roland, thank the System that I've reached you," the Magnificent Donovan Trueheart said with relief. "How runs the System?"

"There is nothing for you to worry about," Roland reassured him. "In your absence, all anti-System factions have been quashed. Food riots are a thing of the past; anyone who does riot has their entire food ration curtailed. Faith in the System is restored. Once again, the System provides and everyone is content."

Donovan Trueheart beamed with pride. "I knew I could rely on you, Roland!" he said. "And now I need your help once more. Things have gone disastrously wrong in the Honeywell..."

"I know..."

The Trueheart frowned; how could Roland know? He chose not to pursue that question.

"I need a skimmer to come and take me off the Earth –"

"The Home Planet, I think you mean," Roland said, reminding him of the official name of Earth.

"Yes, I know that," said the Trueheart, becoming slightly irritated. "Now, can you arrange that for me –"

On the screen he watched the Child Roland stroke his chin, making a great show of pretending to consider the matter. "Well, it may take some time," he said finally. "I have some rather urgent Presidential business to attend to first..."

"*Presidential* business?" asked the Trueheart.

"Oh, haven't you heard?" Roland said, casually. "There's been a minor change of circumstances in the System since you've been away. Seems that someone leaked out a few secrets – destroyed planets, ruined lives, financial irregularities, private vineyards, ever increasing waistlines – that sort of thing..."

"Who?' asked the Trueheart, although he already knew.

"I really have no idea, Your Magnificence," Roland continued, and his use of the Trueheart's official title was now clearly laden with sarcasm. "But it seems that the System wanted a new leader... So I'm sure you'll understand that it might be some time before I can get a skimmer out to you. Although from the looks of things, it seems that you may not need it. You've got company, Donovan."

Roland's face faded from the screen of the smart-box as the Child broke the connection, and Donovan Trueheart looked around at the figures emerging from the shadows. Instinctively, he reached for his gun, and realized that he had lost it in his escape from the Honeywell.

Ganymede strode up to him, followed by his fellow mutants. There was murder in his eyes; there was a knife in his hand. Two mutants grabbed each of the Trueheart's arms; others started to paw at his fine scarlet robes, and poke him in his fat belly.

"You are Donovan Trueheart." It wasn't a question; it wasn't even a statement. It was an accusation.

"Have pity on me," the Trueheart whimpered, as he saw Ganymede raise his knife.

"Like the pity you showed to my people?" Ganymede asked. "The people you experimented upon, carved up, mutated, and then left to die?"

"It was for the good of the System," the Trueheart protested. "To create new life, to push humanity up on to its next stage of evolution, to quicken the natural way of things..."

"To play at God," Ganymede corrected him, and then shook his head. "Humanity will evolve at its own pace, Trueheart. Nature should not be tampered with, as you and your kind have tampered with us. The skies should not rain acid, the rivers should run clean, and crops should grow in fertile soil. And people like you should not be allowed to live."

"*Please...* I don't want to die..."

"It is the natural way of things," Ganymede said, taunting the trembling System President.

"I never meant any harm," he lied. "*Believe me. Know that I speak the truth. I am Donovan Trueheart: believe my True Heart.*"

"Then let us see just how true your True Heart is," said Ganymede, and plunged his knife into the chest of the Magnificent Donovan Trueheart.

Momma Knows Best

It was three days before Shari, Kristas and Cruse returned to the site of the Honeywell. It hadn't been their idea, but rather the suggestion of the mutants they had saved, who had wanted to see if they could salvage anything from the ruin caused when Momma Mercy blew up her base (incidentally one of the biggest explosions in that part of Wessex since the Great Colonial Wars).

Cruse had advised against it, until he had checked the radiation read-outs on board Trueheart's skimmer (which, as the System President had guessed, he had commandeered). The area, so the read-outs told him, were surprisingly free of radiation. He hadn't believed it until one of Momma's cloned Helpers, now released from Momma's control, had told him that most of the power Momma used to run the Honeywell wasn't nuclear, as Cruse had suspected, but solar. It seemed that Momma had no wish to add to the Earth's pollution; after all, it would only be a matter of time before that pollution sank into the ground and poisoned the underground streams, on which the Honeywell relied for its water. Cruse had added that Momma showed no compunction in "polluting" the human species, however.

When they had arrived at the Honeywell, they found that it was in ruins: Momma had done her job well. And while there was some sadness that they couldn't appropriate some of the good things of the Honeywell – the animals, the trees, the flowers, and, above all else, the seeds of the trees and flowers – there was rejoicing, too.

"When I was being operated on, Momma Mercy told me that the Honeywell was the headquarters for all the System's biological experiments," Kristas informed Cruse and Shari. "Its destruction means an end to all the System's genetic research – for the time being at least."

Shari looked over at the mutants they had rescued from the Honeywell; Ganymede and his friends weren't among them and she doubted she'd ever see them again, realizing that they had probably all been killed in the tunnels as they searched for the True-heart.

"It means the end of experiments on the mutants,

too," she added. "At long last they'll be able to evolve naturally, just as nature intended."

"The Inheritors will help them," said Barnaby. "Perhaps there is some way we can make the Earth fertile again, make crops grow..."

"Momma managed it," Shari pointed out. "You need to bore wells deep into the earth, to reach those underground rivers which haven't been contaminated yet." She grinned to herself, and walked over to their skimmer – or rather the skimmer which had belonged to Donovan Trueheart, and where they had stored the Inheritance.

"The Honeywell stretched over most of south-eastern England," Cruse reminded them. "Sections of it must have survived the blast. There will still be plants there, and animals that Momma hasn't mutated beyond recognition. You'll be much safer now – the System increased its presence on Earth because they wanted to track down Kristas and bring him to Momma Mercy. With any luck they'll think he's died in the destruction of the Honeywell."

"We still don't know what happened to Trueheart or Momma, or even Muhajji," Kristas pointed out, as Alice and Casterbridge came to join them. Alice reached out for, and held, Kristas's hand.

"Muhajji was a clone, created purely to track you down with his psi-abilities," Cruse said. "He was an innocent, and had served his purpose in bringing us to the Honeywell. It's better you don't ask what happened to him..."

"And Trueheart and Momma Mercy couldn't have survived the conflagration," Casterbridge said, leaning on his stick. "No one could have..."

Cruse shrugged. He had learned that it was better never to assume anything about any leaders of the System.

Kristas let go of Alice's hand, and bent down to pick something up off the ground. "Look everyone," he said, and showed them what he had found.

It was a blade of grass, fragile, green and indescribably beautiful.

"You see, things can grow in this soil after all," he said.

"But how?" Alice was astonished.

"Who knows?" Kristas said. "Perhaps something to do with the Honeywell? Maybe seeds were blown out when it exploded, and have started to germinate in the soil? But what does it matter? It means that nature is fighting back, that despite all the Donovan Truehearts and Momma Mercys of this world, you can't totally defeat her. Mother Nature's always there, just waiting for the opportunity to come back..."

"And if your theory is right and this soil can support crops again, do you mind telling me just how we're going to raise them, Dreamer?" asked Cruse. "None of us knows the first thing about farming or growing crops!"

"Oh yes we do!" said Shari, who had returned from the skimmer, with several books she had taken from the Inheritance. She passed them over to Kristas who read the titles in wonder: *Robinson Crusoe; Survival Techniques in the Wild; The Natural History of Selborne; Crop Cultivation and Animal Husbandry...*

She turned to Cruse with a look of triumph on her face. "You see, Cruse, the Inheritors were right after all – the Inheritance is a great source of power. But it's not a laser-rifle or a new way to kill people: it's knowledge. Those books, that were saved from whatever library was on the surface before the Colonial Wars, are going to be of much more use to them than a thousand new weapons. It's knowledge that will reclaim the Earth for the mutants and the Inheritors."

Cruse smiled, reluctant to admit that Shari was right, even though they both knew that she was. Instead he joined Alice and Kristas as they pored over the books.

"You've hurt yourself, Kristas," he said, and pointed to the strange rash on Kristas's hand as he turned over the pages. He remembered the rash he had had in the Honeywell, but which had now disappeared. Funnily enough, he remembered Shari saying that she had scratched herself as well. And Barnaby had had a rash too.

"Oh that," Kristas said nonchalantly. "It's nothing.

I must have scratched myself in my sleep, or when I was under anaesthetic and being operated on. Don't worry about it, Cruse... It's just a scratch, that's all..."

"Are you happy, my little darling?"

"Of course, Momma," said the Child Roland – or rather the System President as he was now known – and settled himself into the plush velvet chair in the Presidential office, and sipped at his glass of mineral water. "And it's you I have to thank from the bottom of my heart..."

Momma Mercy waved aside his thanks. "I only did what any mother would do for any of her children," she said. "And you have always been my favourite child, Roland, ever since I first brought you into this world eleven years ago..."

"It's an honour to be Momma's favourite amongst all her Little Helpers," Roland said, with genuine affection.

"It has been a long struggle, but ten years of waiting have not been in vain," Momma said. "At long last you have the Presidency of the entire System, absolute control over every living creature, and Momma can do what she wants."

"I am only here to serve my Momma," the Child Roland professed. "After all, that is why you created me."

"It is sad about the Honeywell, though," Momma said, and wiped a tear from her eye.

"Then we shall create more Honeywells for you, Momma, a thousand Honeywells if that is what you want," the Child Roland promised. "I am only distressed that Shari, Cruse and Kristas, and the Inheritor Barnaby Rudge, those ingrates who broke my Momma's heart and killed her beautiful baby, died in the explosion. They should have been brought to justice."

Momma stood up and walked over to the Child Roland's mahogany desk. There was a small rack standing there, in which four test-tubes had been placed. Momma Mercy picked one out and held it up to the light: it was filled with a blue-green fluid, similar to the liquid that had filled the Other's nutrient tank.

"These are DNA samples from each of them," she told Roland, and smiled. "Contained in them is all the information Momma needs to create a carbon copy of any one of them. Identical in every respect to the original, even down to their memories."

"Momma..." The Child Roland was rendered speechless by the guile and genius of the woman who had cloned him from cells eleven years ago.

"Cruse, Kristas, Shari and Barnaby may have survived the explosion," she said. "But Momma prepares for every eventuality, my poppet. Each of them was away from the others for a period of time, enough for Momma to play her little games. We shall track them down, and then we will show them what it means to upset Momma..."

Momma Mercy turned as the velvet drapes in front of the door were drawn back and a figure strolled into the room. The newcomer smiled at the astonished Child Roland, and then went over and kissed Momma Mercy fondly, like a child greeting its mother.

Momma beamed. "Have you met the latest member of our little family, Roland?" she asked, with evident pride, and hooked an arm around the waist of the new arrival.

The Child Roland opened his mouth but still no words left his lips. The person standing before him was a perfect cloned double, identical down to the smallest feature, of that hated rebel who had caused him and Momma Mercy so much trouble.

"An exact replica, but obeying only Momma's orders?" Roland asked finally and Momma Mercy nodded.

"Ready to do my bidding and strike when the time is right..."

"But how did you get their genetic data?" Roland asked.

"While they were sleeping," Momma told him. "They won't have noticed anything, except perhaps a tiny rash from where I took a few cell samples, but nothing more..."

Momma Mercy sighed and, leaving the side of her new creation, the creature she would send out to wreak her revenge on Cruse, Shari, Kristas and Barnaby, she walked over and kissed the Child Roland on the cheek.

"You see, my darling, they may be ungrateful for all I do for them, but in the end, their Momma truly does know best. In the end, all my darlings will come home to Momma and do her bidding. And Momma does *so* love her little babies. . ."